NORMA TADLOCK JOHNSON was born in Portland, Oregon, and now lives in Washington State with her husband. Mrs. Johnson is the author of several romantic suspense novels for adults, but BATS ON THE BEDSTEAD is her first children's book. She got the idea for the book when her daughter was remodeling an old house and discovered bats in the attic. Mrs. Johnson did some research on bats and found them to be more fascinating than frightening, "in spite of the folklore. I tried to impart some of this fascination in the story."

BATS ON THE BEDSTEAD

Norma Tadlock Johnson

Illustrations by Judith Gwyn Brown

AN AVON CAMELOT BOOK

AVON BOOKS
A division of
The Hearst Corporation
105 Madison Avenue
New York, New York 10016

Copyright © 1987 by Norma Tadlock Johnson
Published by arrangement with Houghton Mifflin Company
Library of Congress Catalog Card Number: 86-27823
ISBN: 0-380-70540-0
RL: 4.6

First Avon Camelot Printing: August 1988

CAMELOT TRADEMARK REG. U.S. PAT. OFF. AND IN OTHER COUNTRIES, MARCA
REGISTRADA, HECHO EN U.S.A.

Printed in the U.S.A.

OPM 10 9 8 7 6 5 4

With love and thanks to my family—
my husband, Bob; my son, Karl;
and my daughter, Janice,
whose house had the bats.

The
House

The first bat came the night we moved into the old
house. He hung upside-down from the foot rail of
my bed. I wasn't scared, not then. It was interesting.
I'd never seen a bat before, although I'd always
collected animals. My zoo, Mom called them, before
we moved and she made me give away the rats and
turn the snakes loose.

I didn't see the bat come but something made me
open my eyes. You know the feeling you get when
you're being stared at. We used to do it in Mrs.
Rockford's fifth grade, back home in Livington City.
We'd stare at kids from behind until they felt the
vibes or whatever they are. It was especially fun to do

it to Karen Sue. She'd get mad and stick out her tongue. Mrs. Rockford would say, "Ricky, whatever you're up to, stop it!" which wasn't exactly fair.

Anyway, that was the way I felt — uncomfortable — like someone was staring at me as I lay in bed trying to go to sleep while my brother Sam snored. Mom says he has to have his adenoids out as soon as we're settled here in Torland. Sam's five, six years younger than I am, and he wouldn't hear it if you set off a firecracker once he's gone to sleep. I know. I tried it once, but it made Dad mad. He said he'd had enough of noises like that when he was in the army.

So that first night in our new house, I didn't try to wake Sam. He isn't especially interested in animals anyway. He likes trucks and bulldozers and anything with a motor in it. And as I said, I didn't know enough yet to be scared. I thought it was just an encounter with some animal species I didn't know anything about. Man, was I wrong!

I stared back at the bat hanging from his toes and peering at me with shiny black eyes. It was confusing to stare at an animal that was upside-down. It shouldn't make any difference; I mean, eyes don't have ups and downs, they're the same shape either way. Still, have you ever looked at things while you're hanging from your knees? The world sure looks different.

I thought of standing on my head, or getting on my knees and looking between them, but that seemed sort of dumb. I tried bending my head sideways but that didn't help, so I gave up and studied my visitor the way he was, upside-down. He was bigger than I thought a bat would be, maybe eight inches from the tip of his head to the claws that clutched my bed. Actually, he hung on the outside, and peered at me through the space below the rail where I hang my socks until Mom catches me. His wings were folded so that they looked like arms, although once in a while he'd flex them and I could see the black skin between the bones. His body was furry and his ears large. Sometimes he opened his mouth as he breathed, and I could see his fangs.

He wasn't exactly cuddly. I had had white rats back in Livington City, and they were sort of cute. Minnie used to run up and down my arms and ride on my shoulder, but I didn't think I'd want to get any closer to this specimen. His face was sinister, with his eyes glinting in the dim reflection from the night-light Sam still insists on having. That's what the bat was, sinister and evil.

We stared at each other unblinkingly. At least, I tried not to blink, but I had to give up. If he ever blinked it was at the same time I did, and I didn't see him do it.

After a while I began to feel uncomfortable, really

uncomfortable. Here was this weird-looking creature at the foot of my bed, staring with those mean eyes. There was no way I could snuggle down in my bed and shut my eyes and go to sleep. I thought for a minute of going to wake Mom and Dad, but I wasn't sure I even wanted to move, much less turn my back on the thing. So I sat quietly, eyes wide open, staring. Everything was still except for the movement of air when the bat flexed his wings. The background noise Sam makes doesn't count. I'm used to that.

The odd thing was that, as we looked at each other, I seemed to know what he was thinking after a while, and I answered him the same way. It was a crazy experience. We weren't talking out loud. At least I wasn't. I reached up and squeezed my lips together to make sure. Still, the conversation went something like this:

"What are you doing in this house?" the bat asked.

"We moved here. Dad got a job and we sold our house and came here."

"We got rid of you humans and we thought we made it perfectly clear you weren't wanted in our house." The bat's eyes narrowed slightly, and he looked even meaner than before. I wondered what he meant by "our" house. Were there more just like him? I supposed so. Bats lived in colonies, didn't they? But how many more? I shuddered. That was an awful thought, to picture a room full of huge, weird creatures who were nasty, threatening, and could talk to me besides.

"It isn't *your* house," I told him firmly, hoping he'd go away. "It's ours. We paid the money we got for the other one to the real estate man. He said an old lady died —"

My words stuck in my throat as the bat chortled and flexed his wings. "We *know* the old lady died," he said.

I felt like someone had hit me in the stomach. I didn't have any air to breathe, and I sat there like a dope, with my mouth open. Then I gasped, and even I could hear my breath go in, ragged and desperate. The bat heard it too, and he knew I was scared. I could tell by the way his mouth opened into a fiendish grin.

"Just consider yourself warned" was the last thing he said. He flexed his wings once more, then swung upward and was gone. I saw only a quick, soundless flash of black, and I couldn't tell where he went.

As I lay back, I felt sweat running down my face and dripping onto the pillow. *Wow,* I said to myself. *I don't believe it!* I kept thinking about my visitor. *And if I don't believe it, will anyone else?*

2

Mom

In the morning, I found Mom on her knees with her head under the kitchen sink. Sam was slurping up a bowl of corn flakes. Ugh. Sam's eating is slobby. "What are you doing?" I asked Mom, adding, "Where's Dad?"

Mom backed out of the cupboard. Her face was red. "I am trying to see," she said, "why the gol-darned sink won't drain!"

Her words weren't exactly gol-darned, but you get the idea. When I say "gol," that's all I say. I'd get in trouble for coming out with more than that. Mom went on, "Dad's already left for work. Hurry up and fix yourself some corn flakes while I change my clothes. I'll take you to school, and then I'll have to come back and struggle with this thing." She slammed the door on the way up.

I sighed as I fixed a bowlful, topped it with brown sugar from the package on the table, and poured milk from the plastic jug. Sam kept on eating. He looks like Mom, with the kind of red-gold hair they call sandy. He doesn't eat like Mom, though.

"Hey, Sam," I asked. "Did you hear or see anything funny last night?"

"Huh?" Milk dribbled down Sam's chin.

"Never mind. And wipe your chin."

After the bat had left the night before and I lay there not able to sleep, I sort of hoped Sam had seen him. I told myself that maybe Sam had just been pretending to snore because he was as frightened as I was. I should have known better. Not Sam.

It didn't look like I'd get a chance to talk to Mom about the bat that morning. Corn flakes aren't my favorite breakfast, but I ate them anyway.

A few minutes later, as we headed toward town in our old Chevy, Mom said, "Sorry I was so snappy, boys. Moving's hard on all of us, and finding the sink stopped up . . ." She didn't finish, but I guess she didn't need to.

"That's okay, Mom," I told her.

As we drove along, I looked around to see what the place was like. There sure are a lot of trees in

Washington, the tall, spiky kind that don't lose their leaves. Back home in Livington City there weren't many trees outside town, only in people's yards. The ones in front of our house were maples and other kinds that turn yellow and red in the fall. I made almost five dollars helping the next door neighbors rake them up last year, but it didn't look like there would be any bucks in leaf-raking around here.

It was hard to tell when you got into Torland. The houses got closer together, but not much, and then we came to the main street. It wasn't very long.

"How'd Dad find a job in such a rinky-dink place?" I asked.

"It's not rinky-dink, Ricky. I wish you wouldn't say things like that," Mom said in that absent tone of voice she uses when she's correcting me. I think she knows I don't listen much. "He drives into Everett every day. That's why he has to leave so early," she went on. She was concentrating on finding the school. "He doesn't have to work all day today though, thank goodness."

"Why don't we live in Everett then?"

"Because we wanted a place with some land and we got a good price." She looked at me as if I should have heard this before, so I didn't ask any more questions.

Sam was bouncing around in the back seat. "Is

that where I'm going to go to kindergarten?" he asked. "Is that my school? Is it? Is it?"

He wouldn't be so excited about it in a few more years, that's for sure. Mom smiled at me, like we knew something Sam didn't. She's kind of pretty, as mothers go. Not fat, or wrinkled, or grouchy looking.

We pulled up in front of an old brick building. Geez! I didn't know they had schools like that anymore. It looked like something out of a story, a story about schools our grandparents went to or something. In Livington City our school was all on one floor, with big windows. This one even smelled different when we got inside — it had a funny smell, sort of musty, or chalky.

We walked down a dark hall somebody had tried to brighten with big streaks of color — red, yellow, colors like that. It was like being inside a rainbow. It looked kind of dumb but I had to admit it helped a little.

Kids of all sizes milled around in the hall as we passed through. Mom stopped a girl and asked her where the office was. Just as the girl pointed, the bell rang. It sounded like Dad's alarm clock. We all jumped since it was hanging on the wall right over our heads, but I jumped the highest. I guess my nerves weren't the best that morning. The bell was a pie-shaped silvery thing. I never saw the one in our school in Livington City.

I felt even more awful when I found out everybody from kindergarten through eighth grade went to school in the same building. I didn't know which was worse, that the sixth-graders weren't the oldest like we would have been back home, or that Sam and I would be in the same building for the next three years. We were going to see enough of each other, living way out in the country instead of in town. Luckily, this year he'd go to kindergarten only three days one week and two the next.

Mom talked to the lady in the office who checked that we'd had our shots and things like that. Finally the woman had an aide take me to my new room. Mom went with Sam. "His first day in school. You remember how important that was, don't you?" she asked, and I nodded.

It seemed like a long time ago that she took me by the hand to Miss Revelstoke's kindergarten. I was so scared I couldn't talk. It didn't affect Sam that way, though. You could hear his chattering as he and Mom disappeared down the hall and around a corner.

I followed the girl, the same one who had pointed out the office to us. She didn't say anything and neither did I. She had long brown hair, a blue blouse, and a blue plaid skirt, and she was at least a foot taller than I was. At least.

I couldn't believe my eyes when we walked into the room. There were rows of those bolted-down desks. I had seen some for sale once in an antique store when I went with Mom. Wow! I wondered what the kids did when the teacher read a story — did they still sit in little rows?

Thirty pairs of eyes stared at me. Or rather, twenty-eight. Two girls were so busy talking they didn't look. At first it seemed like a hundred, but later, after the teacher gave me a desk in the back, I counted them. Thirty, if no one was absent. With me, thirty-one. I'd sure been stared at by a lot of unfriendly eyes in the last twenty-four hours.

The rest of the day wasn't any better. What an unfriendly bunch of kids! As we filed out for recess I could see that half the girls were taller than I was, and they sure thought they were smarter. You could tell. No one asked me to do anything at recess, and at lunch I sat by myself. I wondered what they'd think of me if they knew I'd been talking to a bat the night before.

And the teacher! Talk about grouches! She looked old enough to have taught in the school since the year one. Miss Warren, her name was. I was awfully glad when the day was over.

On the way home, I watched carefully for the corner where we'd be getting off. I'd never ridden a school bus before. Back home our house was six blocks from my school. I once heard about a kid who didn't recognize his stop and stayed on the bus all the way back to school, and the superintendent ended up taking him home. Nobody ever let him forget it. The superintendent, for gosh sakes?

No one else got off at our stop. I recognized it because the house across from our road had a stand for selling corn and squash and things like that. Mom had looked pleased when she saw it as we drove in the day before. Our road is dirt, and you can see the house at the top of a little hill. Like I said, it's old — not at all like our place in Livington City — but it's also kind of neat, with a big porch across the front. Mom had sounded excited about fixing up an old house, but I thought she might just be trying to make Dad feel better about moving. Dad only grunted every time she said anything about it.

Sam and I got off, and the bus pulled away with a roar. It sure didn't look like there would be any kids around, either Sam's age or mine. I was going to miss my friends back in Livington City, and especially Adam. We'd been friends all my life.

The only good thing I could think of about moving was that Dad had said we might be able to get a dog now that we weren't in the city anymore. And it ought to be easy to find replacements for my snakes. A gray and black one crossed the road as we walked up it, but I didn't pick it up. Sam doesn't like snakes much. He was too busy talking to notice, anyway.

"And then Mrs. Green read us a story," he said. "And I already know my colors and my numbers, most of them, and how to print my name, and some of the kids don't." His face beamed.

"That's good," I told him. "Keep it up." He might as well enjoy school while he could. We hurried up the lane.

I was surprised to find Dad home already. His head was under the sink when I walked into the kitchen.

"Hi," I said.

"Oh, hi, Ricky," Dad said, coming out from beneath the sink. "Hand me that wrench, will you?" Dad's face was as red as Mom's had been.

I couldn't think of a good way to say it. "There was a bat in my room last night," I blurted.

"A bat! Oh, Dick!" Mom said. I hadn't seen her come in.

I'm named after Dad, you may have noticed. Richard Paul Engstrom the Third. That's me. He's the Second, or Junior, or something like that.

"Bats aren't uncommon in old houses in the country, Jane," he said. Jane is my mom. "Was your window open, Ricky?" he asked.

"Yeah, sure. I mean, I guess so," I answered.

"Well, then, bats fly at night. They catch insects. Nothing to be afraid of, Ricky. We'll get a screen and it won't happen again." Turning to Mom, he said, "I've just about got this fixed, Jane."

"Oh, I'm so glad," Mom said.

So was I. We'd put up the screen and I wouldn't be bothered again. I felt better than I had all day. I didn't think I'd mention the fact that this bat hadn't been quite the ordinary insect-catching animal. I remembered those sharp fangs. Somehow teeth like that didn't seem necessary for a diet of flies and mosquitoes. And somehow I didn't think ordinary bats talked to people.

"Mom, who lived in this house before we bought it?" I asked.

"We told you. It was an old lady, a very old lady. Her name was Mrs. Lewis. She finally died, quite some time ago, and the house sat empty for a long time. That's why we got it at such a good price," Mom said, "and it's probably why some of the things, like the sink, don't work. Why?"

"Oh, no reason." I lied. I couldn't tell her I'd discussed the old lady with the bat. Even I knew no one in his right mind would believe that. Suddenly I didn't feel quite so good. The bat knew what he was talking about. He hadn't made up the old lady. But what exactly had happened to her? I couldn't decide if I wanted to know or not.

I didn't tell Sam about the bat. He was outside playing, and he hadn't heard me. If the screen worked, and I sure hoped it would, then Sam wouldn't need to know. He gets scared so easily that I didn't see any reason to upset him if the bat never came back.

That night before I went to bed I shut the window, tight. I felt all the way around it to be sure there were no cracks. It was very dark, looking out. A big shrub covered the window. If I had to stay in this bedroom for long, I'd see if Dad would trim the bush.

Even with the window shut I lay awake for a long time, listening to Sam's snoring. I'd sure be glad when he had his adenoids out. Back home we didn't have to share a room. Dad promised that as soon as he could he'd build an addition and I could have my own room again. But in the meantime, I was stuck with Sam and his adenoids.

I woke up early the next morning and breathed a sigh of relief. No bat had come during the night, and Mom had promised to get the screen that day.

15

She wasn't an awful lot happier about a bat in the house than I was. Maybe that would take care of it and I wouldn't see him again.

School wasn't any better, though. Kids here did their arithmetic differently. Miss Warren didn't like it when I told her that the way I did it worked perfectly fine. She didn't like it any better when I told her she had her gods mixed up. She read a story from a red book about mythology, then tried to talk about the ancient Greek and Roman gods. I told her that Mercury and Zeus didn't belong together but she didn't believe me. I'd always enjoyed reading about mythology back home in Livington City. Somewhere still packed in a box I had a book that explained it all if Miss Warren would listen. Anyway, what good would that do? Her red book probably told all about it if she really read it.

The smarty girls still had their noses in the air and the boys all knew each other. They'd probably known each other since they were born, maybe even in the same hospital, just like Adam and me. I'm pretty good at ball games and wished they'd give me a chance, but nobody asked me. I watched carefully when kids were playing soccer and football at noon, and I kept hoping they'd notice me standing there. But nobody did. So I sat down and read and kept to myself.

Once again, I was glad when the day was over.

Sam was still happy enough with the school. He didn't know any better. He chattered away as we walked up our road. I tuned him out and said "Uh-huh" once in a while to keep him happy.

Mom had milk and cookies for us in the kitchen, so things were getting a little bit back to normal. The kitchen is much bigger than the one we had in Livington City. The cupboards are old-fashioned and made of wood, and Mom says she likes them better than the fake plasticky stuff in our other house.

"I bought the screen for your window, Ricky," Mom said. "It's in your room."

I crammed a cookie into my mouth and went to look, and Mom followed. The screen slid in two sections and fit in the bottom part of the window when it was open.

"That should keep out any bats, Ricky," Mom said. "When we're not so busy, I'll have Dad check the attic, and we'll get rid of them if we have any up there."

Sam came into the room after his bulldozer. "Come on, Ricky," he said. "Let's build a town. I found a neat dirt pile out in back."

Mom winced. Sam likes to play in the dirt, and I knew she wouldn't appreciate the way he looked when he came in; she's a neat mom, though, and she didn't say anything.

I said, "Okay." What else was there to do? Actually it was kind of fun, and we stayed out there a long time. We made roads and parking lots, and I found some blocks of wood behind an old shed which we put in for houses.

I hadn't realized it was so late when Mom called us for dinner. Dad was home and had changed to his work clothes for building shelves in the basement. It was only a little basement, under part of the house, and already it was mostly full of our junk since this house was so much smaller than the one in Livington City.

"I'm putting your stuff on this shelf, Ricky," Dad said after dinner, showing me what he'd done. "Now at least you can get at your books and things. We'll build you a room as soon as we can."

I checked my microscope to be sure it hadn't gotten broken and pulled out a couple of books I thought I might want. "Thanks, Dad," I remembered to say.

I really didn't expect the bat that night. He hadn't come the night before, and now the screen was in. Still, I was relieved in the morning when another night had passed and no bat. After about four nights, I was beginning to think I had dreamed it after all.

I was wrong. And the next time he came, he brought friends.

3

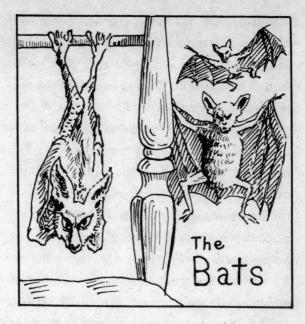

The Bats

"Oh, no!" I thought, with an awful sinking feeling. I felt heavy, as if I were glued to the bed. I knew before I looked that the bat was back. The same uncomfortable feeling of being stared at pounded against my brain. The vibes. This time the sensation was even stronger. I hated to open my eyes. I had to force them open — but I had to look. You know, like a horror movie when it's so gross you begin to wish you hadn't come.

Mom doesn't like me to go to horror movies. She says they give me nightmares, and anyway, she doesn't approve of them. I used to sneak away to one once in a while with my friends or see one on late TV when I was staying overnight with Adam. His mom didn't care. I wondered what Adam would think of a talking bat.

Finally I opened my eyes halfway, and peered out through my lashes. No wonder the vibes were so strong. Three bats had come this time. Voro, as I suddenly knew Bat Number One was named, hung in the same place on the foot rail.

His buddies were at least as big and mean as he was. Bat Number Two hung from the picture of a lion and cub that's always been on my bedroom wall. He had to bend his head up and backwards to look at me. It gave me a crick in my neck to watch him. Bat Number Three swooped around the room. He swished right toward my head, like a dive bomber.

"Hey, cut it out!" I cried, ducking. When I looked again he was settling on the foot rail beside Voro. He slowly folded his wings in sections, watching me without blinking all the while. He was, of course, upside-down. What a strange way to spend your life. Maybe that's what made the bats so mean. From the nasty way the two new ones looked at me I was sure that they were just as bad as Voro, even if he was the leader. Now there were three sets of eyes glaring waves of hate in my direction.

"How'd you get in?" I sneaked a look at the screen. It was still there, in the window.

Voro sneered. "You can't keep us out. You didn't really think a simple little thing like that would do the trick, did you?" I had. At least, I'd hoped so — but I suppose, deep down inside, I had known it wouldn't keep them out if they were determined to get in. Voro studied me with his glittering dark eyes. "Why are you still here?"

"Oh, come on," I said. "My folks *bought* the house."

"The old lady thought she owned the house, too."

I felt cold sweat spring out again, all over. My heart thumped against my chest. I bit my lip as I stared as Voro. His face had weird folds of skin and it looked like he had four ears, two smaller ones tucked inside the huge outer ones. It sure was odd studying him upside-down. I still wasn't used to it. It was as if my mind had to translate what I saw, like I was listening to a strange language.

I didn't say anything. What could I say? I could ask what happened to the old lady. If I dared. I glanced over at the sleeping Sam. I could — Bat Number Three rose up, spreading his wings threateningly as if he, too, were reading my mind. No, I couldn't. I lay still.

"Well, what did they say?" Voro demanded.

"Who?"

"The big humans. Your parents."

"Oh. Well, I told them a bat came, and they got that screen."

The other two spread their wings, their eyes menacing, then settled down again. I lay even more still, keeping my eyes on them nervously.

"What did they say about leaving the house?" Voro demanded. "When are you going? We can't be patient forever!"

"I didn't tell them," I admitted. I couldn't lie. These creatures knew what I was thinking.

"*Didn't tell them!*" all three bats screeched. The sound bounced from wall to wall like an echo. Bat Number Three started swooping around the room again. I ducked under the covers.

"It won't do you any good to hide." Voro sounded very angry. "Tell them. *Tell them!* You are to leave this house, or you'll be sorry!"

I stayed under the covers. I mean, would you have come out? I tucked the blankets tightly around my neck and head and hung on. He said it wouldn't do me any good to hide, but what else could I try?

After a minute or so I could feel the vibes growing weaker, like the sound of a train disappearing. I lifted a corner of the blanket and looked out with one eye. They were gone. Over in the bed in the corner, Sam muttered and turned over. Then his snores started again.

What was I going to do? Sure, I'd tell Mom and Dad. I had to. But tell them we had to move, when we just got here? Was there any chance they would believe me? And if they did, what could we do? I wondered if the real estate agent would return our money. Maybe it wouldn't be too late to go back to our house in Livington City. I didn't think there were bats in Livington City; I'd never heard of any.

I couldn't get to sleep. I definitely wasn't looking forward to morning.

4

Voro

Breakfast the next morning was normal, if you can call it that when my stomach felt all scrunched in a lump and my eyes were scratchy from lack of sleep. The sink was working now, and we had orange juice, and Mom was drinking coffee. She had made oatmeal, which I like even less than corn flakes, but that was all right because I wasn't hungry. I poured milk from the jug and took a spoonful of brown sugar. Maybe that would make the stuff taste better.

"Ricky!" Mom snapped. "Don't put so much sugar on your cereal. You'll ruin your teeth!"

My teeth weren't my biggest worry at the moment.

"Mom," I began, ignoring her. It wasn't easy to say what I had to say. "Mom," I began again, "the bats came back last night."

That stopped her. She put down her coffee. "Bats? More than one? Are you sure, Ricky?"

"Of course I'm sure." What'd she think? That I'd made it up? And I hadn't even told her the bad part yet, about the bats talking — and threatening.

"Well, I'll have Dad check tonight. There must be a hole somewhere. Now, hurry up. You'll miss the school bus."

Sam had already gone out the door, and I could see him halfway down the driveway. Like I said, he's eager. I tried again. "Okay, but Mom, about the bats —"

"Ricky, you don't have time to talk. Finish up your cereal, brush your teeth, and *go*. You overslept this morning. You can tell us about the bats tonight."

I nodded. I had overslept, but anyone would have, after the night I'd had. I'd just as soon wait for Dad anyway. He listens better. Besides, I wasn't exactly in a hurry to tell the folks we had to move because the bats said so. I left the oatmeal, brushed my teeth, grabbed my book and my lunch pail, and left. I was late. I had to run the last part down the driveway while Sam got on the bus.

The bus was about half full. The older kids rode

in the back, and Sam had already sat down with the little kids in front. I picked a seat by myself in the middle.

School that day was the same. I managed to stay out of real trouble. Miss Warren said I wasn't paying attention and she was right, but nothing else happened. I tried doing arithmetic their way and it worked okay. Once I heard someone behind me talking about a bat and I about jumped out of my skin, but it was Miss Warren he meant. I could see what he meant, but she was no competition for Voro — no way!

We had a library period, and the school library was neat, with lots of books I hadn't seen before. I looked at the ones about animals. There weren't any about bats.

"Ricky," Miss Warren said in my left ear. "Are you looking for something special?"

"Oh, uh, well, I wondered if there was a book about bats," I mumbled.

"Let's check with the librarian. If there isn't, she can get one for you." She led me up to the desk. I felt silly, but everyone else was busy looking at books. "Do you have anything about bats for Ricky?" she asked the lady.

"Bats," the librarian said to herself. "No, I don't think so. I'll check with the central library and see what we can get. Anything special you want to know?" she asked.

"Uh, I suppose what they look like, each kind, I mean."

"Oh, so you can identify them?"

"Yeah, I guess so." I thought for a second. "And what they eat, you know?" I thought I'd feel better to find they didn't eat kids. I was sure I'd heard somewhere about blood-sucking bats, besides in my imagination. Voro and his buddies sure had the teeth for it.

"I'll try to have something for you the next library period," she said, smiling.

"Thanks — thanks a lot." I felt like I was doing something a little bit useful by looking them up, although I'm not sure why. I told myself that maybe the books would tell how to get rid of bats.

I found a super book on snakes and a mystery that looked okay. On the school bus going home I didn't see anybody from my class except a couple of girls. I read the book about snakes and almost missed my stop.

Dad got home late that night. I waited until he'd had a beer and read the sports page. He gets mad if anything interrupts him before he reads the sports page. Even Mom doesn't tell him things, like about the car breaking down or me getting in trouble, before he's had his beer and read about the Sea-hawks, his favorite team. I don't know why they're his favorite team. They make him mad too. The trick is not to get in trouble on the same day the Seahawks lose. Mom hid the car for three days the time she dented the fender because the Seahawks had just lost a game by doing something stupid in the last thirty seconds. As Mom said, we all walked on eggshells for a little while.

So I sat kicking my heels while he read and drank. Finally he sighed, drained his can, and laid down the paper.

"Okay, Ricky," he said. "I can see you want some-thing. What is it?"

I sighed too. "There were bats in my room again last night, Dad. Three of them."

His bushy eyebrows went up. "Now how in Hades did they get in?" he asked, getting up. "Come on, we'll go look."

I trotted along behind him. "Get my flashlight, will you, Ricky?" he asked. "It's next to my bed."

I found the flashlight and took it to him in my room. He used it to check along the baseboards, be-hind the furniture, and last, in the closet. He climbed on a chair and shone the light on all the corners of the closet ceiling. He pushed the clothes back and looked behind them.

Finally he backed out, shaking his head. "There

isn't any way they could have gotten in, Ricky. Are you sure you weren't imagining it?"

"Of course I wasn't imagining it!" I was mad. "Do I go around imagining things?"

"No, not usually." He sounded like he was thinking about other things already as I followed him down the hall. I had to get it over with. "Dad, there's something else."

"What?" He kept moving toward his recliner.

"Dad, I know this sounds funny, and I know you may find it hard to believe, and I didn't want to tell you, but one of the bats — I can understand what he's thinking, and he said we had to get out of his house." I finished with a rush. I also ran into Dad, who had stopped suddenly.

Mom was sitting in her chair, and I saw them look at each other. Mom's face had a peculiar expression, like when our dog got run over in front of the house. That was a long time ago but I still remember. I didn't see it happen, but that's when Mom said we couldn't get another dog as long as we still lived in the city.

"Ricky —" she said.

"Ricky —" Dad said. I saw him frown at Mom, and she stopped. "Son, I know this move's been hard on you," he said. "It has been for all of us, with me losing my job and all. So now you're having nightmares. It's understandable."

I shook my head. I hadn't dreamed about Voro, or his friends. They'd been there, just like the picture of the lion and cub on the wall, and Sam in the other bed. I'd even pinched myself to make sure I was awake. "They were *there*," I insisted.

"Now, Ricky," Mom said. "Be reasonable. Dad checked, and there's no way they could have gotten in."

"You've got to believe me!" I said. "Voro — that's their leader — Voro said we had to move. He said this was their house. He — he threatened us!"

"With *what?*" Dad said in that sarcastic tone he uses when he's getting mad. "Bats eat insects. They're good to have around. What do you think they're going to do, eat you?"

Since that was exactly what I was afraid of, I didn't say anything.

"If it will make you feel better, Ricky, I'll get some mothballs, and we'll put them up in the attic. I've heard that discourages bats," Mom said.

I nodded glumly, and left. Mothballs weren't going to get rid of these bats, that I knew. Voro was too tough for mothballs. But I'd done what he'd asked, I'd told Mom and Dad — and made them think I was nuts. What else could I do? Maybe that would satisfy Voro. I sure hoped so.

Not much happened the next few days. I kept telling myself Voro would know I'd told my folks and

leave me alone. Mom looked at me strangely every
once in a while. Dad was cheerful. You know that
make-believe cheerfulness grownups get — the kind
they have when they tell you it won't really hurt at
the dentist's? Or when they tell you that you can't
go to camp this year because they don't have the
money, or that you're going to move? Dad kept calling me "Son" and clapping his hand on my shoulder.

To escape, I asked Mom if I could go for a hike
and see what the country looked like. It was Saturday and I didn't much enjoy being in my bedroom
these days. Pushing trucks around with Sam didn't
seem like much fun, either.

Mom fixed me a lunch and asked if I was sure I
wouldn't get lost. What a dumb question. I hadn't
gotten lost since the time I walked off the end of a
switchback on a Cub Scout hike. Anybody could
have done that. An animal trail led straight ahead.
Just because all the rangers had had to look for me
and it got in all the papers and everything, she never
let me forget it. Gol, that was four years ago, and I
don't do dumb things like that anymore.

So I put my lunch in my backpack along with a
can of pop, and I set off.

One thing sure was different from Livington City.
When you got outside of town there, you came to
farms right away. Here I never came to anything I
would call a farm. Everybody had a place like ours,

with a little bit of land around the house. The houses weren't all the same, though. I got on one road where they were awfully big. A man standing at his mailbox asked me who I was and where I was going, and I don't think he was just being friendly. But when I got away from there I saw old houses like ours, and new ones, and what my folks call tin houses.

I think some of the people thought they were farmers. I saw a couple of cows, and lots of horses, and several places selling corn like the one across from our house.

Finally I saw some woods that had a FOR SALE sign posted along the road. Woods around here have a lot of junk growing in them — ferns and bushes and berries. You can't just walk anywhere like we could at home. These woods, though, had a path. I followed it, and after a while I came out at a neat clearing with a little stream, where I ate my lunch. Mom had put in a piece of chicken left from last night's dinner. She must have been feeling sorry for me.

I watched a garter snake weave out of the woods and across the grass. He was big and pretty. Green like the meadow, with a red stripe. I didn't see any other animals, but I pretended there were bears and deer and coyotes in the woods.

After I'd finished eating, a cloud moved across the sun and it started to get cold. I decided it was time to go. In fact, when I got out of the woods it looked like it might rain. I headed home by what I figured was the shortest way, on a road I hadn't been on yet.

Just before I came to Fir Drive, our street, I saw a dirt road leading to a tiny green house, which was even smaller than ours. A sign that said PUPPIES was tacked to a fence post.

While I stood there wondering if it meant they had puppies for sale, a pickup came alongside me.

"Do you want a puppy?" A woman leaned across from the driver's seat. She was young and had long brown hair.

"I — my Dad says maybe — I don't know." Suddenly I thought of Voro. What would bats do to a puppy? Scare him half to death, that's for sure. And maybe worse than that. I swallowed hard.

"Come up and see them anyway." She had turned the pickup into the dirt road and now she opened the door on my side. "They're awfully cute. Hop in."

I thought for a second. But what harm could it do to look? I got in beside her.

"They're some kind of spaniel mix," the woman said. "We don't even know what Lady, their mother, is. She's a nice dog. We just want homes for the puppies where they'll be taken care of. They should all have good dispositions. And as I said, they're cute."

They sure were. It seemed like there were a jillion, but the woman said there were only eight. Lady was a golden color, but the puppies were all colors. I especially liked one that was spotted, and he liked me. He licked my face.

I sat on the ground while the puppies climbed all over me. Pretty soon the woman said, "I have to go in now, but stay as long as you like. Just shut the gate when you leave." I nodded.

I hated to go, but pretty soon I decided I should. I didn't think I'd tell Mom and Dad about the puppies. They'd said we could have a dog, but getting one now didn't seem like a good idea. I'd worry about him too much, and anyway, wouldn't it make Voro and his buddies even madder? I had a hunch they didn't like dogs.

I patted the spotted puppy one more time, then shut the gate and left. It was lucky I did, because it started raining as soon as I got home.

The kitchen smelled good, but Mom and Dad weren't there. I could hear voices, and hammering, and Dad swore. I followed the noise. They were both in the bathroom. I'd forgotten they said they were going to start remodeling it today. It was kind of a funny dark room.

Mom stood on the stool and Dad on a stepladder. They were holding a sheet of something over their heads, and they had opened up the walls.

"Wow," I said. You could see wires and pipes and boards in the walls.

"Good, you're just in time," Dad said. "Get up on the ladder and help us hold this wallboard. I can't hold it and nail at the same time."

Mom's face was pained. "Hurry up," she croaked.

"Couldn't you —" I started to ask.

"Hurry *up*," Dad said.

I scooted up the ladder while Dad stood on the side of the tub. The wallboard was heavy, even though I was only helping. Pretty soon Dad said, "Okay, that should be enough nails to keep it in place," and I let go. Mom rubbed her arms.

"Couldn't you stick a board under it or something, to hold it up?" I asked.

Dad quit hammering and looked at me. "I'm afraid it would break —" Mom began.

"No, wait," Dad interrupted. "I could make a cross-piece and use it to brace . . . Good thinking, Ricky. You've got a head on those shoulders." He reached down and mussed up my hair. "You can leave, Jane, and I'll see what I can come up with."

I followed Mom out to the kitchen. She poured me a glass of milk and took two cookies out of the glass jar she keeps them in. "Did you have a good hike?" she asked me.

I told her about it, all except for the puppies. I

had just finished the cookies when Dad bellowed, "Come on, both of you. Let's get this other sheet up."

He'd made a brace, which he had me shove under the middle of the sheet while Mom and he held it up. It did help. He had the piece nailed in in no time. I felt good. For a while I even forgot the bats.

After dinner, though, I remembered. I stayed up as late as I could, a long time after Sam went to bed. Mom said, "Ricky, you've been yawning for the last hour. Go to bed." Dad looked at me the way he does, and I knew it was no use arguing.

The room was dark except for Sam's night-light. I switched on the lamp. Nothing could wake Sam. With the light on it seemed like a perfectly ordinary room. I undressed slowly and climbed into bed. I was sure that the bats would be back tonight. I put off turning out the light as long as I could. At last I flicked it off and dove under the covers. It felt safe under there. Maybe that's what a caterpillar feels like in his cocoon, snug and secure. But the caterpillar isn't really safe; his enemies know he's there, and it was the same with me.

Right away I sensed the vibes that meant Voro had returned. I ignored him. Maybe he'd go away if I stayed under the sheets.

"Come out. I want to talk to you." Voro's words pressed into my brain.

"I don't think I want to talk to *you*."

"Did you tell them?"

"Yes."

"Good." Voro sounded surprised. "What did they say?"

"They didn't believe me."

"Didn't believe you!" The angry words beating inside my head sounded loud enough to wake Sam, even though I was convinced they weren't really shouted.

I sat up in bed, and I was angry too. "What did you expect? They think I'm having nightmares, that's what. Who'd believe me? Talking bats! Maybe I *am* dreaming!"

"You're not," he said smoothly. "I assure you you're not." He sneered in a toothy grin.

I looked around. This time there were five bats, hanging on the picture, the bed, and the molding up near the ceiling. I dove under the covers again.

"That won't do you any good. You know that," Voro said. He was quiet for a moment but I knew he hadn't gone away. I could tell. I cowered under the blankets and waited. "All right," he said. "You get another chance. Only one more chance. Tell them again. Make them believe you. Because if you don't . . ."

I sensed that he was flexing his wings again in that frightening way. I stayed under the covers; there was nowhere else to hide. Soon I felt the vibes going

37

away, fading the way they had the last time. After a moment I peeked out. The room was quiet except for Sam's snores. Didn't that kid wake up for anything?

I lay awake for a long time. What was I going to do? What a predicament. I'd heard Mom say "Between a rock and a hard place." That was me. If I didn't tell Mom and Dad, Voro and his buddies would get me. I didn't know how they'd do it, but I managed to think of a few horrible ways.

I knew blankets over my head wouldn't save me. Would they gnash me with those wicked-looking fangs, or did bats really suck people's blood? I had a vision of my body lying there, all white and drained of blood, with the bats chortling and flying away, and Mom and Dad and Sam finding me in the morning, and everybody crying. I could see Mom sobbing, "Oh, if only we had listened to Ricky," and Dad with a red nose, holding her, and Sam hanging on to both of them and wailing like he does when he gets upset.

Would they believe me then? And what would they do? Move back to Livington City when it was too late to save me? My room would be awfully empty.

But what if I did tell Mom and Dad that the bats had come back again with even worse threats? I could picture their faces with that worried, scared look.

Not worried and scared about the bats, but about me. They'd think Richard Paul Engstrom the Third was off his rocker, completely crazy, and I couldn't blame them. I guess if anybody had come to me with a story like that, I would have thought so, too.

What was I going to do?

5

Dad

Hammering woke me up. The sun shone on my wall and I knew it was late. Sam's bed was rumpled and he wasn't in it. Usually I don't sleep through Sam's getting up. He's noisy. Worse yet, he's cheerful when he wakes up. I was glad he was gone. I especially didn't need Sam's cheerfulness that morning.

I thought about the night before. The last thing I remembered was hearing the rooster across the way crow. He lives where the people sell corn. Dad said one of these days we were going to have rooster stew, but I didn't really believe him. Then I thought that maybe the bats were considering having Ricky stew. My stomach gave a lurch.

I sure felt tired. I turned on my stomach and tried to go to sleep again. Pound, pound! I pulled the pillow over my head. It didn't help; the bathroom was right through the wall from me. My bed jumped every time Dad hammered.

So I got up. I looked in the bathroom. The sink was gone. Dad was hammering wallboard where it had been. "Oh, just a minute, Ricky," he said. "The water's turned off. I'll be done here in a second, and I'll turn it back on."

I went looking for Mom. She was stirring something on the stove. "Sorry if we woke you," she said over her shoulder, "but you slept awfully late and Dad needed to get started." Then she looked at me, really looked at me. "Ricky!" she said. "What's the matter? You look terrible. Don't you feel well?"

"I didn't sleep too great, Mom," I admitted. I had decided, during the long, dark, lonely hours that I lay awake, that I'd rather face Mom and Dad than the bats. "I — I — the bats came back." I finished in a rush. "Five of them this time."

"Oh, Ricky!" she said, looking woebegone. "I don't know what to say."

Sam was eating breakfast, and he stared at me, his eyes wide and confused looking. Dad walked in just then and Mom told him, "Ricky says the bats came back last night." She had a funny tone of voice, sort of flat.

"I suppose they talked to you again?" he said in that sarcastic way he has.

"Yeah — yeah, they did," I mumbled. I had to get it over with. "They said we had to move."

Mom and Dad didn't say anything and I couldn't look at them. I knew it was hopeless. I don't know why I'd even bothered. If Mom and Dad wouldn't believe me — and I didn't blame them too much — there wasn't anyone else. I left to get dressed.

"You can use the bathroom now, Ricky," Dad said quietly as I left, and I nodded.

Nobody mentioned bats all morning. After breakfast I asked Dad if there was anything I could do to help. Now he looked at me as if he really thought I was sick. Just because I offered to help! But I didn't have anything else to do, and anyway, it had been sort of fun yesterday.

"You can help me pound nails in this sheet if you want," he said. He showed me how. I only missed a couple of times, and the white powdery stuff inside dribbled out. "That's okay," he said. "When we tape we can cover it up."

Finally he said, "I think that's all you can help me with now, Ricky, but we're going to build your room next, Mom and I decided. I think you can help a lot with that if you'd like. We had to do this first because the pipes were leaking. Why don't you find Sam? He's kind of lonesome."

I said okay, but I wasn't really in the mood. I went into my room and read but I felt too uncomfortable. I kept looking for things that weren't there. I sure couldn't concentrate.

I went outside and played on the dirt pile with Sam for a while. He'd made the town bigger and had found a whole sack of play people Mom and Dad bought for us once when we were on a trip. I'd forgotten about them. There were men and women and children and dogs and even some farm animals. He said his town was Livington City. It didn't look much like it. Livington City was flat, not hilly. Maybe Sam missed it more than I thought. He had some good friends there, kids he'd known all his life just like I did.

"Ricky," Sam said suddenly, not looking at me as he pushed a truck up a hill, "were there really bats in our room last night?" His voice was quiet and very small.

I swallowed and pushed the dirt where I was building a road. I didn't want to scare Sam. But there was no use lying. If I did, he'd probably tell Mom and Dad, and then they'd really be confused and mad. And anyway, Sam might as well know. He'd have to eventually. "Yes, there really were bats there last night. And the other nights."

He was silent for a moment, still not looking at me. Then he said, "Did the bats really talk to you?"

"Yes," I answered.

"Oh."

He didn't say anything else about it, and I played there with him for a long time.

Later I decided to visit the puppies. I didn't tell Sam where I was going. Maybe someday I'd take him to see them. They weren't very far away, but just then I didn't feel like talking about them.

There wasn't anyone around when I walked into the yard of the house where the puppies lived. They all yipped and bounced against the chicken-wire fence of their pen. I thought I'd better ask if I could go in.

I knocked on the door and the same lady answered. "Hi," she said. "Did you decide you wanted one of the puppies?"

She looked disappointed when I said no. "But I came to see if I could play with them."

"Sure," she said. "Come any time, as long as you always close the gate. I know you did last time. By the way," she added as she shut the door, "one of the puppies went to a new home this morning, and another will be going tomorrow."

I hurried to see if the spotted one was still there. He was, and he was glad to see me. He licked my face and climbed all over me. He had a fat little belly. He was clumsy and fell over his own feet. It reminded me of Sam when he was first learning to walk. It was hard to tell that one puppy was missing; it seemed as if there were so many of them. They were a lot of fun. I wondered if Mom and Dad would let me get a female someday so we could raise a batch of puppies. The spotted one was a boy, though.

"Hey, boy, would you like to go home with me?" I asked, and he whimpered and licked my chin. I squeezed him and swallowed hard. "You wouldn't want to come," I whispered. I put him down and left the pen, shutting the gate behind me.

"Where have you been?" Mom asked when I walked into the kitchen. She didn't sound mad. She trusts me pretty much, even if she does remind me about getting lost with the Cub Scouts.

"Oh, just on a walk," I said, and she looked at me sort of funny.

After dinner I put off going to bed as long as I could. Sam had gone a long time before, and you could hear his snoring clear in the living room if you listened. Dad looked over at me during a TV commercial. "Shouldn't you be in bed?"

"Uh, yeah, I guess so." I didn't get up.

"Tell you what, chum," Dad said, "how would you like it if I slept in your bed tonight? You could make out on the couch, couldn't you?"

"Sure! You bet!" Suddenly I felt great. I supposed the bats could come and find me in the living room, but I didn't think they would. The bedroom was their place. I could feel it as soon as I walked into the room, and nowhere else in the house. Dad went downstairs and got my sleeping bag, and Mom spread it on the couch. I got my pajamas and changed in the bathroom.

Mom and Dad said they didn't mind going to bed early — they were tired from remodeling — so we all sacked out. I wished the bats would come while Dad was in there, only I felt mixed up about it. I didn't want anyone else to get scared the way I was, but if Dad saw them everyone would believe me. As soon as I had that thought, though, I knew it was hopeless. Voro wouldn't come that night. I felt it in my bones. It was me he'd decided to pick on and me he'd talk to. After all, he could have gone to Mom and Dad in the first place. He and his friends wouldn't come as long as Dad was in the bedroom. I knew it for sure.

I wondered if Mom and Dad would let me sleep on the couch every night. Nah — they often watched TV after I went to bed. This time they'd said they were tired, but they wouldn't be tired every night. Well, at least I'd be able to get a good night's sleep and not have to worry too much about bats. In the morning I'd figure out what I was going to do.

6

RiCKy

The next day was a good one. For one thing, I had
slept well — didn't hear a thing. Then at breakfast
Mom told Sam and me that we would have to stay
in a motel for at least two nights. The plumber was
going to tear out the toilet and the beat-up old bathtub that morning, and Dad would put a new floor
down when he got home from work. The next day
somebody was going to put vinyl on top of that, and
the day after that the plumber would put in a new
toilet and tub. What they were going to do didn't
matter. What was important was that we would be
staying in a motel two nights. I felt so relieved that
even school didn't seem so bad.

It was library day again and the librarian had two books on bats for me. She said one of them was an older encyclopedia and wondered if it wouldn't be too hard for me. Miss Warren, who was standing nearby, said, "Oh, no. Ricky's a good reader. He won't have any trouble with that." She surprised me. I didn't know she thought anything I did was good. You could never tell from the expression on her face.

The books were great — if you like to read about weird things, that is. I thought Voro and his friends were repulsive until I looked in those books. Wow! If someone with the wildest imagination in the world set out to draw pictures of the ugliest, scariest creatures he could dream up, this is what he'd end up with. There were bats called *spear-nosed* and *leaf-chinned* and *fringe-lipped* and *hammer-headed* and *tube-nosed*, and the worst thing was that they all looked like their names.

They were even weirder when I started reading about them. There were sucker-footed bats with discs on their feet that stuck to things. There were even bats that the army had tried to use to carry bombs back in World War II. The idea was to make the bats go into hibernation by keeping them really cold, almost freezing. They'd have bombs attached to them, and then, when they were dropped from parachutes, they'd wake up, chew off the straps with those sharp teeth, and fly away, leaving the bombs behind. Imagine! Scientists sure have some far-out ideas! It worked pretty well, according to the book, but someone invented the atomic bomb around then and the war ended.

The only bad thing about the day was that Miss Warren kept yelling at me to do school work instead of read. Actually, yelling isn't the right word. She never yelled. She just said things in that icy cold way that made you jump. Her voice reminded me of Voro's. Mean and demanding and confident. I wasn't the only one Miss Warren scared. Nobody else wanted to do anything wrong either. It was the quietest class I'd ever been in. That's one reason I was able to read so much.

I said that was the only bad thing; I forgot the other. I was reading how most bats eat insects, like Dad said, when I came to a section about vampire bats, which feed on blood. It was saying that they live in the tropics, but about then Miss Warren got really nasty and said she'd take my book away if I didn't pay attention. I could hardly wait until after school to read that part.

Our house was a mess when I got home, with tools and stuff from the remodeling sitting all over. There were even a new tan-colored toilet, bathtub, and sink sitting in the living room. There was no room to sit down and read. Mom had brought suitcases up from the basement, and she told Sam and me to hurry up and pack what we'd need for a couple of days. "Don't forget your pajamas and toothbrushes," she said as she dashed out of the bedroom.

Pretty soon she came back to be sure we had everything, especially that Sam did. We were okay. I'd reminded Sam about his underwear. His suitcase had mostly toys. You'd think he'd be in the motel for a week instead of at school most of the next two days.

Mom had dinner ready the minute Dad walked in. She and Sam and I left for the motel in the old Chevy right after we ate. Dad was already ripping things up in the bathroom when we left. While we were in the car, I suddenly remembered the puppies. I'd meant to go see them after school. Maybe some of them would still be left when we got back home. I hoped I would see the spotted one again.

The motel room was one of those ordinary ones with two big beds, a small table and two chairs near the window, a TV, and not much else. At least it was on the ground floor and we didn't have to lug our junk up a lot of stairs.

As soon as we got our suitcases and an ice chest in the room, Sam took out his trucks, Mom turned on the TV, and I flopped on the bed with my book. I turned to the place I'd marked with a gum wrapper. *Vampire Bats*, it said in darker print than the rest. Vampire bats, it continued, don't really suck blood.

They make slashes with their sharp teeth, then slurp up the blood with their tongues. I didn't think I cared for that method any better than sucking. I pictured Voro's sharp fangs and shuddered.

Vampire bats are about three and a half inches long and live in Central and South America. There were maps in the book with the range of each kind of bat marked in pink. Vampire bats clearly did not live in Torland, Washington, U.S.A. Voro was not a vampire bat, at least not the kind they were talking about in my book. I kept reading.

Hmmm. Carnivorous bats. They eat meat. That sounded even worse, especially if the meat were human flesh — like that found in an eleven-year-old kid. I read on. Carnivorous bats, according to the book, eat mice and small birds and things like that. They didn't sound like much of a threat, and anyway they lived in Africa and Asia. I read some more. I clearly had not found Voro and his clan. What I did find was that there are over 2,000 kinds of bats. Actually, the books didn't agree on this; one said 2,000 and the other 800. Either way, at the rate I was going it would take me a long time to work my way through the bats.

About that time, Dad showed up. "Hi, gang," he said, after Mom let him in the door.

"All done?" Mom asked him.

"Blankity no," he answered. I can't say what he

really said. One of those forbidden words. I don't see why grownups can say them, and say them where kids can hear them, and yet they get mad if kids use them. Anyway, he went on, as he collapsed on the bed, "I'll go over really early and finish up. I've already called the boss and he says I can be late. That was one blank of a job getting the bathtub out. It may have been old, but it weighed a ton." He rolled over on his stomach and Mom rubbed his shoulders.

"Poor dear," she said.

I went back to my book. Suddenly I came to something that might be important. I sucked in my breath. "Mom," I asked, "what did the old lady die of?"

"What old lady?" she asked.

"The one that lived in our house. Did she die of rabies?"

"Rabies!" Dad yelled as he sat up. "What in tarnation are you reading?" He came over and grabbed my book. "Oh — I see." He sounded as if he couldn't decide whether he was mad or worried. I've heard the tone of voice before. Like the time I climbed up a cliff at the lake and got stuck.

"Look, Ricky," he said. "Yes, bats can carry rabies. That's why we have our animals get shots for it. But it's rare, very rare, and the only time anyone worries about it is when they see a bat — or other animal for that matter — acting really strange. So there's no reason to worry about it."

Personally, I thought Voro *did* act really strange. "Why don't people get shots?" I asked.

"Because presumably they have enough sense to stay away from animals that are acting peculiar. A dog or cat doesn't. They might cheerfully jump on a bat flopping around in the yard in daylight."

"How peculiar? What do they do?" I could still picture Voro hanging upside-down, snarling and flexing his wings, not to mention talking. If that wasn't peculiar behavior for a bat I don't know what was.

"Oh, they foam at the mouth, and stagger, and maybe lose their fear of humans. Anything unusual like that."

That didn't help a lot. Voro sure didn't have any fear of me. "But how did old Mrs. Lewis die?" By now I really wanted to know.

Dad shut my book with a snap. Even Sam looked up. He hadn't been paying any attention. Mom looked like she was going to cry. "Ricky," Dad said firmly, "that is enough. Absolutely enough. She died in bed of a heart attack, like almost anyone would who had survived to the age of ninety-three. Now I want you to quit torturing yourself over a — a bad dream. I don't like to tell you what you can or cannot read. You've used excellent judgment so far. But tonight I don't want to hear one more word about bats, and I don't want you to read any more either. Do you understand?"

I nodded as he rubbed his hand over his forehead like he was in pain. I assumed he meant not to read any more about bats that night. He hadn't said anything about the next day, or later. I'd just be careful not to talk about bats around him. I didn't blame him, although you'd think he could try to believe me. I didn't usually go around lying, and why should I start now?

I brushed my teeth and put on my p.j.'s, and then Sam and I climbed into bed together. If I couldn't read, I might as well go to sleep, I figured. Anyway, Mom had turned off the TV and she and Dad were getting ready for bed, too, with Dad grumbling about how early he had to get up as he set the alarm. "Remind me to reset it for you," he mumbled as he put the clock down.

It was only later, after the lights were out and I lay listening to trucks rumble by — it was much noisier than at our house — that I thought about how my heart had thumped so hard when Voro came. If I'd been ninety-three, mightn't I have died right then of a heart attack?

And what if the bats had really attacked her? I could picture swarms of black flopping, shrieking, angry bats all over the poor woman, who tried to defend herself with her feeble old arms as she lay in bed. But, in my vision, it was *my* bed she was lying in. I wondered if anyone had even bothered to look for tiny fang marks. As Dad had said, no one would have been surprised to find a ninety-three-year-old woman dead. They probably wouldn't have examined her very closely.

I sure would like to know which room the old lady had slept in, but I decided I'd better not ask Dad, or Mom either. Besides, I was pretty sure I knew.

7

Spot

I haven't said much about the weather. That's because it had been perfectly ordinary — not too hot,
not too cold, with only that little bit of rain once.

When I think about it, that's odd. Everyone back
home had told us we'd grow webbed feet, like ducks.
They talked about liquid sunshine, and how people
who lived in western Washington thought they were
having a heat wave if the sun shone more than one
day. The sun had been shining most of the time
since we got to Washington, but no one seemed
particularly excited. You'd hear people say "Nice
day" and things like that in the grocery store, but I
couldn't see that anyone thought it was out of the

ordinary. Maybe it wasn't going to be as bad as people back in Livington City had said after all.

When we woke up the next morning, though, it was pouring. You could hear water gurgling down from the gutters and spilling into drains in the parking lot. Sam and I peeked out between the curtains because Mom wanted to keep them shut. She said she didn't want people to see us eating breakfast since we really weren't supposed to do that in a motel, but I didn't see why anyone would care. What were the table and chairs there for anyway, if people weren't supposed to eat?

We had corn flakes again, but we each got a piece of a sugar bun. Of course, Mom doesn't approve of sugary things like that for breakfast but I guess she wanted to make breakfast a little better that day. We'd had cold corn flakes an awful lot lately. She also gave us money to get a hot meal at school. Most of the time we took food in our lunch boxes because Mom said she could give us a lot better lunch for the money. Usually the lunches she made were pretty good, but it was fun to buy the hot lunch once in a while. I hoped it would be something I liked.

"I guess we'd better go shopping for rain gear after school, boys," Mom said as she dropped us off at school. "You'd get pretty soaked if you had to walk up our road in this. And tonight," she added, "we're going out for pizza."

Sam yelled "Hooray" and I guess I did, too, because that's our very favorite dinner. It gave us something to look forward to.

All day I read about bats every chance I got, but I was more careful than before. I had a hunch old lady Warren wouldn't just slam my book shut like Dad had done if she caught me reading it when I wasn't supposed to. Not after the day before, when she'd gotten mad several times. She'd probably take the book away and give it back to the library.

I still hadn't found any bats that sounded like Voro. Maybe his group had just moved to town. I could ask him if I saw him again. *When* I saw him again. With no ifs-ands-or-buts, like my grandmother used to say, I knew that I *would* see him again, and I was afraid it would be as soon as we got back to the house. Voro probably thought he'd gotten rid of us, and he wasn't going to like having us show up again.

I kept trying to shove thoughts like that away, though. After all, I was safe as long as we stayed in the motel, and I wanted to enjoy it while I could. In the meantime I'd keep reading, because I felt somehow that I might find an answer to my problem in the books. If I at least found out what kind of bats they were, maybe I could call someone and ask how to get rid of them.

It rained all day and Miss Warren seemed grumpier than usual. Maybe it was because we spent our recess and part of our lunch period inside. You'd think she'd be glad not to have to stand outdoors, although I guess she didn't have to all the time. I think the teachers took turns. She probably wanted to drink her coffee and be peaceable, like Sam always said.

It was still pouring when Mom picked us up after school. We dashed out the front door and into the Chevy. The windshield wipers were going squeak-squawk like they always do, with the right-hand one acting like it wasn't quite going to make it. I don't mean to say that it never rained in Livington City. It did, and usually hard, but it just didn't happen very often. The wipers complained every time there, too.

Mom drove to a Penney's store on the main street. It looked like all the Penney's stores I'd ever been in, although maybe smaller. It sure was smaller than the one in Livington City. Mom bought us each a yellow raincoat and a yellow hat with a brim that was bigger in back than in front, and black rubber boots with buckles. "My little fishermen" she called us as she paid for the gear. I wasn't sure I liked that. I knew what she meant because I'd seen pictures of fishermen on the big boats in Alaska and Maine and places like that, but I didn't think I liked being called one because I know I'd never be a fisherman. I don't like to kill things even if I do like to eat them. In fact, I think I'd be what they call a vegetarian if it were left up to me. I don't even like to think of things dying. Me, for instance. Or the puppy if I brought him home, and the bats didn't like it and attacked him.

We went back to the motel to wait for Dad. There weren't many people on the main street. Penney's hadn't had very many shoppers in it either. It seemed to me that the stores might as well close and let everyone go home. People don't go shopping on a night like that if they can help it.

The motel had a lot of people staying there, though. You could tell from all the cars even if you didn't see anyone. The No VACANCY sign was lit up and everybody was shut inside the little rooms. I wondered why they were there. I was sure we were the only ones who'd had their bathroom ripped out. Most of them were traveling somewhere, but why on a rainy night in September?

We hung our wet raincoats in the shower and did our usual — Mom watched TV, Sam played with his cars, and I read my bat book. Mom glared at it and asked if I didn't have homework to do, but I said no, and she didn't say any more. Actually, we did have a paper assigned. But it wasn't due for a couple of days, and as for the arithmetic — well, that I could do at lunch or recess. It would probably rain, and we never did arithmetic until after lunch.

60

Sam was the first to hear Dad in our station wagon. He has a real knack for engine noises. When he was three he'd say "Daddy's coming" when he heard the car a block away. At first no one believed him, but he was always right. He could even make out the next door neighbor's Volvo and the pickup across the street.

That night he lifted his head and listened a minute, then said, "Here comes Dad." We heard the swish of tires pulling up outside, and Mom unlocked the door. I quickly tucked the bat book under my pillow. No use asking for trouble.

Dad looked happier than he had the night before when he came through the door. He held his thumb and finger together the way he does when he means everything's okay, then kissed Mom and said, "Hi, gang. Ready for pizza?"

We said sure and we put on our new raincoats, and pretty soon we were all sitting in the pizza parlor. Then Mom asked, "How did it go today, Dick?"

"Much better," he said. "The plumber will install everything tomorrow and we can go home."

Mom said, "Thank goodness." I don't think she likes watching that much TV.

Sam said, "Hooray!"

I didn't say anything. But I don't think anyone noticed because the waiter brought our pizza just then.

We were finishing munching and Mom was cleaning up the stringy bits of cheese that Sam got all over when Dad said, "I have a surprise. The plumber lives just around the corner from us, on the next street, and his dog had a batch of pups. She had eight, and he's been looking for homes for them — only has four left. How about going to look at them, Ricky?"

As I said, Sam isn't much into animals, but even he looked excited and said, "Are you going to get a puppy, Ricky?"

I didn't answer either of them right away and Mom asked, "What kind, Dick? We don't want one that's too big."

"Oh, they're not. The mother's some kind of spaniel mix and they're not sure about the father, but the puppies don't look like they'll be too big."

I remembered Spot's big feet and wasn't so sure about that. I hadn't meant to name my favorite one, and especially something dumb like Spot. It sounded right out of that old-fashioned first-grade reader with Dick and Jane. I suddenly realized those were Mom's and Dad's names, too, and that would be sort of funny.

I was smiling to myself when Dad startled me by saying, "You haven't answered, Ricky. How about it? Do you want to go look at them after school?"

"Oh, uh, I've seen them, Dad," I finally came out

with while I tried to find an answer. "I saw them when I went for that hike. And I went back once and played with them."

Mom looked at me in amazement. "You never mentioned it, Ricky. How come?" She knew me pretty well.

"Oh, I just didn't think of it." Finally I said, "Thanks, Dad, but I don't think so. Not right now."

I couldn't tell him I didn't dare get Spot because I was afraid the bats would hurt him. Dad knew, though. I could tell by the strange way he looked at me. He's pretty smart sometimes.

Dad just shrugged his shoulders and said, "Okay. It's up to you."

8

Sam

The next day was horrible. Actually, things started
getting bad the night before, while we were still at
the motel. I could hear Mom and Dad whispering
about me over in their bed when they thought I was
asleep. I couldn't really hear them, but I heard
"Ricky" and "bats" and even "crazy." I think Dad
said "It's crazy," but I'm not sure he didn't say "He's
crazy."

I guess because they were so upset about me, they
had forgotten to set the alarm. So everyone got up
late, Dad went rushing off without breakfast, Sam
and I had to gulp ours down, and we were late to
school. Then our class had arithmetic first. I ask

you! What made old lady Warren pick that day to do arithmetic first? She said it was because we were going to have a movie in the afternoon. I, of course, hadn't done my homework, and Miss Warren didn't like that at all. The movie turned out to be a dumb thing on foreign countries, probably made by someone who wanted to sell tickets for an airline. There were lots of cows standing in fields. I'd seen cows before. I kept sneaking looks at my bat book, but Miss Warren caught me and took it away. The only good thing was that she gave it back after the movie was over, without saying a word.

Time was getting short for me. I still hadn't found anything useful, though I was sure learning a lot about bats. In fact, you might say I was now an expert. But I still hadn't found any bats that matched Voro. One of the books said there were little brown bats and silver-haired bats around our part of Washington, but neither kind was really scary. Some looked like mice or rats with wings, and I was used to that after Minnie and her babies. Those bats wouldn't scare me.

After school I took the bus home. My feet dragged as I walked up our road. It wasn't raining anymore, but there were puddles in places I wouldn't have expected, and the black sky looked as if it would rain again any minute.

Mom hugged me as I walked in the door, something she hardly ever did anymore. "Come see our new bathroom," she said.

It did look nice, sort of. It hadn't been painted yet and there were white streaks and blotches on the wallboard where the cracks and nails were covered up. But the new tan tub, sink, and toilet were in, and there was a new floor that looked like brick only it wasn't really.

"We're going to wallpaper and build cupboards," Mom said. "But we don't have to hurry for that. At least the plumbing doesn't leak anymore."

I dreaded night coming. My room now seemed to be so filled with evil that it hit me like a blast of cold air when I opened the door. Sam obviously didn't feel it. He made happy noises as he rummaged around looking for something in a drawer. I couldn't stand it. I left.

I didn't ask if Dad would sleep in there again. What good would it do? The bats were after me, only me, and they would just wait if I talked Dad into sleeping there. After dinner, once again I put off going to bed as long as I could. Mom walked into the room with me, talking softly, although I don't know why because she knew even a bomb wouldn't wake Sam. She didn't talk about bats. Neither of us did, but we were both thinking about them. I watched her to see if she felt the atmosphere inside the room, but her face didn't change. She looked worried, but she always did these days when she looked at me. It made me feel bad because I didn't want to worry her and Dad. I hugged her back when she tucked me in.

"Oh, Ricky," she said as she squeezed me, and she left fast. I think I saw her wipe her eyes as she went out the door and I felt even worse.

After she left I waited. And I waited. There was no point in trying to sleep until they came. I could feel the evil come and go, like waves at the beach. Each time, when I was about ready to scream from the force, I'd expect to see Voro; but then it would go away, and I'd lie back with sweat dripping from my face. He never came. I finally went to sleep, again about the time I heard the old rooster across the way.

The next day was Saturday. I thought about going to see the puppies but decided it would just make me feel terrible. Maybe they'd all gone to new homes by now. I hoped Spot went someplace where they'd be good to him.

After a while Dad asked Sam and me if we'd like to go to the lumberyard with him. We said sure. It's one place we both like. Sam likes to watch that machine they use to move stacks of lumber. He says he's going to drive one someday. I just like to go because — well, I guess I like the smell of the place, and the neat stacks of things, and anyway, this time Dad was ordering lumber to start the new bedroom for me.

He said I could help build it, and we spent a long time there ordering the stuff. The man said they would deliver it on Monday. We took a lot of things — nails in brown bags, insulation and such — in the station wagon, and I helped Dad unload. Then I helped him begin shoveling dirt to make the place for the foundation.

I stayed up that evening as late as I could again, but I fell asleep on the couch and woke up only when Dad carried me into the bedroom. The evil didn't seem quite as strong that night, and I began to hope that maybe the bats wouldn't come anymore. I had been certain they would the night before, our first night back from the motel, but they hadn't. Maybe they knew I'd done everything I could.

I was hopeful when I went to bed Sunday night. I'd felt better all day after having slept the night through for a change. Most kids don't think about things like that. I sure never had. Until the bats came I had always slept like a log, or so Dad always said. But when you don't sleep you feel awful. So on Sunday I helped Dad all day and went to bed at the usual time. The vibes weren't there, and I even went to sleep. I figured they weren't going to come, at least not that night. Again, I was wrong.

I woke up with a humming sound hammering into my head. I shoved my head under the pillow, but it didn't make any difference. It wasn't a sound, but a vibration. I could hear it, or feel it, just as strongly with the pillow pulled tightly over my head as without. I wanted to keep hiding and not look, but something kept pressing me, forcing me out from under the covers. Finally, I decided I might as well face it, so I rolled over, pulled off the pillow, and slowly opened my eyes.

The room was full of bats. There were big bats, little bats, and in-between bats — and all unfriendly. They hung along the molding up near the ceiling. They hung, three or four of them, from every picture. This time they were even draped all over Sam's bed. He slept on, snoring.

As usual, Voro hung from the foot rail of my bed. Several of his buddies were there, too, upside-down of course. I thought they probably could do as much damage from either direction. Their wicked fangs looked like small knives. I don't know how I knew which one was Voro, but I did. He resembled the others, but was maybe a little bigger and meaner. He was their leader. I could feel it.

Everywhere I looked, glittering eyes glared at me. The bats kept changing positions. They'd unfold their wings like umbrellas, then swoop over to another spot where they'd fold up again and hang with their fierce-looking claws. While I watched several swooped right over my head with their claws extended, and I winced and ducked although there was nowhere to go. I couldn't sink into the mattress, much as I would have liked to.

All the time, the humming pounded into my brain. I realized now that the evil feeling I'd felt before was that noise, only not so loud. I didn't even try to go back beneath the covers. What was the use? I had known they'd come, and now I knew they would get me, only I didn't know exactly how. I shut my eyes. I didn't want to know, and with my eyes closed maybe I wouldn't know until it happened.

It was the worst thing I'd ever experienced, as I lay there expecting to die. Voro didn't say anything. The humming grew louder, and I felt the air blow against the skin on my face as they flew overhead. I didn't move a muscle as I waited. My heart pounded and I was sure the blanket above my chest was going up and down with each beat.

Finally I couldn't stand the waiting anymore. I opened my eyes again and said, "What are you going to do?" Even to me, my voice sounded like a croak.

"*What are we going to do, what are we going to do?*" the bats chorused as they flexed their wings.

"Why did you come back to the house?" Voro demanded.

"What can I do about it?" I was pleading now. "It isn't *my* house, it's Mom and Dad's. And no one believes me. I *told* you they wouldn't!"

"*Make* them believe you! *Make them believe*

you!" he screeched. "Because if you don't —" He stopped for a moment and became very still, obviously thinking. The other bats quieted down, too, waiting. My pajamas were soaked with sweat, and I shivered as I, too, waited. All of a sudden I started to laugh, and I couldn't stop. I laughed and laughed. All I could think of was how funny my bedspread must look, with me shivering and my heart pounding.

"Stop laughing!" Voro shouted, and I did. Just like that. It didn't seem funny anymore. "*One week* we'll give you. And then —" His leer was the most totally evil look I'd ever seen or imagined.

"*One week, one week*," the other bats chorused in the background like an evil accompaniment.

"And then," Voro continued, "I think we'll begin with your brother. There will be no further warnings. If you don't want your brother to suffer, you'll persuade your parents to move. They'll do it. They'll have to. And, just to persuade you —"

He took off, diving straight for my head. The other bats were right behind him. I screamed and dove under the covers. I screamed and screamed —

The next thing I felt was something shaking my shoulder. I tried to jerk away. "Ricky, Ricky! Stop that!"

It was Dad. He pulled the covers off my head. "What's the matter, Ricky? A nightmare?"

"The bats," I hollered, "the bats!" I couldn't stop

shaking and tears were running down my cheeks, which was dumb because I hadn't cried since I was a little kid, but I couldn't help it.

The light was on and I looked around. The bats were gone, every one of them, and there was no sign that they had ever been there. I shook my head. No wonder no one believed me. One picture frame had been knocked a little crooked, but that happened all the time anyway. I wondered why the picture hadn't fallen off the wall, with so many big, ugly bats clinging to it. Mom was there, too, and even Sam was sitting up looking at me. Wow!

"The bats said we had to go or they'd — they'd get Sam." I whispered the last. I didn't want Sam to know before he had to.

Mom looked at Dad. "I told you Ricky wasn't —" She stopped in the middle of her sentence. "Now we have to get help." Dad nodded. "Tomorrow," Mom said in that tone of voice she uses when she means business.

She turned to me. "Do you want to spend the rest of the night in our bed?" It had been a long time since I'd slept with them, but it sounded awfully good that night.

"Go back to sleep, Sam, honey," Mom said, and she went over and kissed him. "Ricky's just been having nightmares." I swear that kid was back asleep before we even got out of the room.

For a minute, as I lay between Mom and Dad, I wondered about the "help" Mom said they'd get tomorrow. Help in getting rid of the bats? How? I didn't know what they could do, but it made me feel better. So did snuggling in their warm bed. I went right to sleep.

9

The
Bats

The next day at school when the aide came to get me and said I was wanted in the principal's office and was to bring my coat and things, I was surprised. I followed the girl with her swishing plaid skirt, worrying. I hadn't been to the principal's office here. Not yet. I had been several times in Livington City, but I couldn't think of anything I'd done here serious enough to get me in trouble.

When I saw Mom and Dad I was even more scared, but the principal just said, "Your mother and father have an appointment for you, Ricky, and they came to get you."

I knew it was about the bats, knew it right away

from the expressions on their faces. They were all alike, all three faces. Even the principal's. They looked worried . . . and something more. They looked at me like I was a — a freak or something.

On the way to the car, I asked, "Are we going to see someone who's an expert on bats?" I was afraid I already knew the answer.

"Not exactly," Mom answered. "Just someone we think can help."

Oh, brother. Now I knew I was in trouble. I settled in the back seat and my heart sank. The night before, when Mom had said they were going to do something, I thought she meant they were going to get rid of the bats, or maybe even go back to Livington City. Instead they were taking me to see someone who didn't know anything about bats. A fat lot of good that was going to do. As if it were all in my head or something. I didn't ask again where we were going. I just sat in the back seat of the station wagon, glum, while Dad drove and Mom rattled on the way she does sometimes. It occurred to me that Dad must have taken time off from work, and that made me feel even worse.

The door of the office where we went was covered with names, all followed by Ph.D. or M.D. or some other combination of letters. We had to wait in uncomfortable chairs inside, with Mom flicking through the pages of a magazine she obviously wasn't looking at and Dad staring straight ahead while he drummed his fingers on the back of the chair beside him. I just sat there, swinging my legs.

Finally a lady came out of one of the doors and said, "I'm Dr. Jerison. How do you do, Mr. and Mrs. Engstrom? Ricky?" She shook hands with each of us. She looked nice enough, but she had eyes that made you feel she saw way down inside you. I'd hate to have someone with eyes like that for a teacher. Then she said, "I'd like to speak to your parents first, Ricky, if you don't mind."

I nodded and sat down. I turned the pages in my bat book, but it didn't help. I'd read it all now. Several times. And there was nothing in there that sounded at all like my bats. Still, I kept flipping through the book.

When Mom and Dad and the doctor came out, they looked serious. At least, Mom and Dad did. The doctor looked the same as before. "All right, Ricky," she said. "If you'll come in now."

I followed her into a room. I'd expected an office but it wasn't. It was more like a living room, with comfortable chairs and a low table. Mom and Dad had obviously been drinking coffee. Dr. Jerison picked up the cups and said, "Would you like something to drink, Ricky? I think there's a soda." I nodded, and she disappeared through a side door with the cups, then came back in just a minute with my drink.

"Now, Ricky," she said, "I'd like you to tell me about yourself."

I looked at her in surprise. She hadn't said anything about bats. I didn't answer.

"Tell me about your friends, your school," she suggested. "Do you like school?"

"Uh — it's okay, I guess," I told her.

We went on like that. She still didn't say anything about bats. Somehow, though, I got to telling her about Livington City and my friends there. She was kind of a neat lady. It seemed as if she understood how I felt about the move although she didn't say so. She stood up.

"Aren't you going to ask about the bats?" I said.

"Do you want to talk about them?" I nodded and she sat down again. "Tell me about them," she said.

I told her everything about them, what Voro had said, and how there were more of them each time.

"How do you feel about the bats?" she asked.

"*Scared!* Sort of fascinated, too," I admitted. "I sure wish they'd go away."

She smiled, then stood up and put a hand on my shoulder. "That's all we have time for today, Ricky, but I'd like to talk to you again."

We went out into the room where Mom and Dad

waited. They made arrangements for me to come back on Friday. Dr. Jerison was a nice enough lady, but sitting and talking to her was a complete waste of time. If Mom and Dad wanted me to come, though, it wouldn't do me any good to complain. I had until Sunday, and if it made them feel better to have me talk to her, I would. They couldn't say afterward that I hadn't cooperated.

We stopped at the grocery store and then went home. I didn't feel like doing anything. I went into my room. Today it seemed perfectly ordinary. No strange feelings, no bats, just two beds with blue bedspreads, a chest of drawers, a desk and chair, and the pictures. Mom must have straightened the one. The lion and cub looked out at me as I lay on the bed. I wished they could talk. They'd have seen what was going on in the room.

I lay there thinking about everything that had happened since we'd moved here. I hadn't wanted to come. I didn't think Mom and Dad had wanted to come very badly either, except Dad had to have a job. Sam didn't really care, even if he missed his friends a little. He's happy all the time. What a lucky kid. But that would all change next Sunday when the bats went after him. Maybe everyone would believe me then. When Sam told them about the bats, too. *If* Sam could tell them afterward. I swallowed hard and felt awful.

That was absolutely, totally, the worst twenty-four hours in my life. I remembered how I'd felt the night before, how scared I'd been. I'd worried all day about what I was going to do, and then, the last straw, Mom and Dad had taken me to a shrink. There was no getting around it. Instead of believing me and doing something useful about getting rid of the bats, they'd taken me to a psychiatrist or a psychologist or whatever that lady was. She hadn't acted as if she thought I was crazy, only listened, but everybody knows you have to be nuts to go to someone like that. Was I nuts? I had to admit that if someone had come to me before this happened with a story about talking bats, not only would I not have believed them, but I might — just might — have thought they were crazy, too.

Nobody believed me. That was worse, almost, than being scared of the bats. Mom and Dad didn't believe me, I was sure the school principal didn't, and I doubted the shrink did.

What was I to do? I lay on my back, my arms behind my head, and stared at the foot rail, the molding around the ceiling, the picture on the wall where they had all hung. I was afraid to sleep in the room anymore, but I couldn't, just couldn't, face the looks on Mom's and Dad's faces when I talked about the bats. Would they send me away? Maybe that was the best thing that could happen. Send me to wherever they lock up crazy people. I'd be safe. The bats couldn't get me there.

But that wouldn't help: if I weren't there the bats would go after Sam. They had said they would. Poor Sam. He was too little to help himself. No, I'd have to try to keep my mouth shut. I wouldn't talk about them anymore. I was no nearer to a solution, although I'd done everything I could think of. Now I'd just have to wait for whatever was going to happen. Maybe I could talk the bats into going after me instead of Sam. Would everyone believe me when they found my body sucked dry of blood, lying on my bed next Monday morning? Tears slid out of the corners of my eyes and dripped down into my hair. I shut my eyes.

"Ricky?" Sam's voice made me open them again. He had slipped into the room and stood beside my bed.

"What, Sam?" I wiped my eyes quickly, pretending I was rubbing them.

"I wanted to ask you, Ricky. When the bats come — would you wake me up? I want to see them."

"Huh? You want to see the bats?" I looked at Sam, his sandy gold hair all messed up and his face as dirty as usual. I sat up and grabbed him. He must really have thought I was nuts because I hugged him. "Sure, Sam, of course. I'll wake you up."

Sam believed me. Would Mom and Dad if Sam said he saw them too? That was important, very important. But it didn't matter as much as the fact that someone believed me. I felt a lump as big as a rock in my throat.

"You're a good kid, Sam," I told him.

10

RicKy

I didn't feel much like going to school the next day, but I didn't see how I could get out of it. I waited for the bus alone. It was one of the days Sam doesn't go. When the bus came I said "Hi" as usual to Mr. McDonald, the driver. He said "Hi, there" back to me but didn't smile. Mr. McDonald never smiles. He's not grumpy or anything, although he doesn't let kids get away with anything on his bus. It's just that he always has the same expression under his Mariners baseball cap.

Also as usual, I looked for an empty seat in the middle of the bus. As I headed down the aisle I heard "Pssst!" A redheaded kid I'd seen before gestured for me to sit next to him. I sat. We were almost in the back of the bus.

"What's your name?" he asked, sort of looking me over.

"Ricky Engstrom," I answered. "What's yours?"

"Mark. Mark Stone. I live back that way." He pointed. "You new?"

"Yeah."

"Where ya from?"

"Livington City," I told him.

"You're in Miss Warren's class, aren't you?" I nodded, wondering how he knew. "I had her last year. She's not too bad." That sure surprised me. "I guess you're in seventh grade, then," I said.

"Yeah." The bus rumbled on. After a while he said, "My sister's in your class. Margaret."

"Oh." That explained a lot. Margaret must be one of the two girls in my class who rode this bus. She looked like him, now that I knew. She had dark hair but they both had freckles and their faces were the same shape.

We had only a couple more stops, and then the bus pulled up by the side of the red brick building.

"See you," Mark said as we got off. Some other boys were calling him. I walked across the playground and sat down, leaning against the building. Mark was already kicking a soccer ball with the guys.

The day went pretty well at school. Miss Warren

told the class that I had been right about the Greek and Roman gods, and she gave us a lesson on how both ancient Greece and Rome had had the same gods only called them by different names. I felt good about that. It couldn't have been easy for her to say she was wrong.

At noon we went outside after lunch, and Mark saw me right away. He stuck two fingers in his mouth and whistled. Gol, I wished I could make a noise like that! I decided I'd have to get him to show me how. He waved his arm, meaning "Come on over." I went. There were seven guys, two kids from my class and the rest older. "You ever played soccer?" Mark asked.

"Yeah. Yeah, I have," I told them. I kept my face straight, but it was hard. We had a soccer league back home and it was probably the sport I played best.

"Well, come on," Mark said. "You can be on my side."

We played until the bell rang and if I do say so, I did all right. I went into Miss Warren's room with the two kids from my class, Steve and Jerry.

The bats were on my mind all day but somehow I managed not to think about them too much. That was what I had decided to do — think about them as little as I could. Now, unless I got a brilliant idea, I'd try to forget about them and enjoy the time I had left. If I could. It seemed to be working that day.

84

I was already on the bus after school when Mark came along. He sat beside me. "You want to come over to my place?" he asked.

"Sure," I said. Then I remembered. "But I'll have to stop and tell my mom where I'm going." She's fussy about that. She knows I won't do anything dumb, but she sure gets mad if I forget to tell her where I'll be. Dad, too.

"I'll get off with you," Mark said, "and then I can show you where I live."

Mark wasn't much of a talker, but it was nice to have company. Mom said I could go to Mark's after she questioned him about where he lived and everything. She gave us milk and cookies.

We were walking down our road still eating cookies — they were good, chocolate chip — when Mark said, "You ever see any bats?"

I almost choked. He whopped me on the back. "Bats?" I finally managed to croak out.

He looked at me sort of funny. "Yeah. The old lady who used to live here said she had lots of bats. She even claimed they talked to her. Can you imagine? She was pretty batty, though." He laughed. "That's a joke. Get it?" He was so busy poking me with his elbow and laughing that he didn't see my face. I was glad.

I didn't answer and I guess he thought he'd been so hilarious that there was no need to. As I said, he wasn't much of a talker and I was glad of the chance to think while we walked along.

So the old lady *had* seen Voro and his buddies! I wondered who she'd told. If I could find out, maybe I could talk to them, or get Mom and Dad to. Maybe they'd believe me when they knew she had seen the bats. They'd have to believe me.

The only thing was, I didn't want to ask Mark. I didn't know him very well yet. I had a feeling that maybe we were going to be friends, but he obviously thought the idea of talking bats was totally crazy. And what if we didn't become friends? He might be the kind who would tell the whole school, and that would be a disaster. I imagined what it would be like to have all the kids pointing their fingers at me and laughing. *"Hah, hah! Ricky talks to bats! Hah, hah!"* I decided to keep quiet for now, and wait and see. I still had five days.

Mark didn't turn on the road toward the house with the puppies, but went straight ahead. I felt sad as I looked in that direction. I didn't see the sign on the fence anymore. I hoped they had all gotten good homes.

We left the open fields and got into a wooded section. I was wrong about the leaves around here not turning color. There were some bright red bushes that Mark said were vine maple. They looked really pretty next to the dark green trees, which I'd learned in school were called Douglas firs. They were named after some guy from Scotland who came to the Northwest just to study plants. That was way back when the only people here were Indians, more than a hundred fifty years ago. It must have been fun for him to come to a place where no one else had looked. He could have named everything after himself if he'd wanted.

Mark's house wasn't very far from ours, and I was surprised I hadn't seen him wandering around the neighborhood. The house was in the middle of a bunch of Douglas firs, and it looked like part of the forest itself. The wood was unpainted and natural color, and the roof was made of cedar shakes.

"Mom wants to cut down some of the trees," Mark told me, "but Dad won't let her. She says she's the one who's here all day and she wants some sunshine. Dad says there's no sun anyway, so we might as well look at the trees." He laughed and threw a stone into a mud puddle.

Mark's mom was nice and she gave us milk and cookies, too. Neither of us told her we'd already had some. Her cookies had raisins in them. We fooled around in Mark's room for a while, but his sister kept pestering us.

"Margaret thinks you're cute," Mark said. "I

heard her and her silly friends. *Cute!*" He looked at me and collapsed laughing on his bed. He might not talk much, but he sure laughed a lot.

I laughed, too, but I was embarrassed. Girls never pay any attention to me because I'm short, and I don't care anyway, but Mom says I'll grow. She says Dad did all his growing between thirteen and fifteen and he's tall, so I shouldn't worry. The next time Margaret stuck her head in the door I pretended to ignore her, but I sneaked a look. She wasn't bad looking.

Pretty soon I said I had to leave. Mom had said Dad was going to have a surprise, and I wondered what it would be. Something to do with my room, I supposed, but I wanted to see. I said goodbye to Mark, and he said he'd see me the next day. Mrs. Stone said to come back. Margaret didn't say anything.

It didn't take me long to get home. Dad's car was parked out in back so I knew he'd arrived. I hurried up the driveway.

Sam and Dad came out of the little gray barn behind the house. "Hurry up, Ricky!" called Sam. Dad shushed him, but his face was excited too. I was getting more curious all the time. I ran the last part of the way.

Dad opened the door of the barn while Sam jumped up and down beside him. There, wriggling

88

his hind end because he was glad to see me, was Spot. I dropped down and hugged him, and he kissed me with his wet tongue. He was so soft and warm and squirmy. I sure was glad to see him again.

"The plumber was going to take him to the pound. They'd found homes for all the rest. I figured you wouldn't want that to happen," Dad said.

"The pound — oh, no! Of course not — not to Spot." Even risking bats was better than that. I just wouldn't have him sleep in the bedroom at night, especially the night I expected the bats to come.

It might make the bats even madder that we'd gotten him, but I didn't see how they could be much more upset than they were. Anyway, if Spot went to the pound he'd really be in trouble. He was awfully cute, but I knew the pound was full of cute dogs who needed homes. It was worth it to take a chance to save him from being locked up in a cage and maybe killed.

11

Spot

It was only later I figured out that Dad must have been making that up about the pound. Spot was the best looking, nicest, and friendliest of all that batch of puppies, and he couldn't have been the last one chosen. I bet Dad had planned it the whole time, and had him picked out, and maybe the lady had even told him I'd been there. I didn't care.

"I see you've named him already," Dad said.

"Oh, well, I — I called him Spot because he had so many, and then I remembered Dick and Jane and Spot —"

Dad laughed. "Spot it is. He was obviously meant for our family."

I hadn't noticed Mom coming out of the house, but she was standing next to Dad and he had his arm around her. She looked happier than I'd seen her since Dad first lost his job, back in Livington City.

Sam sat on the floor next to us, and Spot climbed all over him, too, but he kept coming back to me.

Pretty soon we had to go in and eat dinner, and Mom let him come on the back screened porch. "He's not entirely housebroken yet," she said. "You'll have to train him, Ricky. And he'll have to sleep there or in the barn until he is," she added.

I was glad I didn't have to say that I didn't want him in the bedroom at night, so I said, "Sure, Mom. He's smart. It won't take him long."

Mom had to remind me about my homework after dinner, but she let Spot stay in. "We might as well start now on housebreaking him," she said. He only peed once, which I thought was pretty good for such a young dog, and he seemed to understand why I put him out the door for a minute. Later, when I had finished my homework, he even seemed to ask to go out, and I took him to the back yard.

I hated to say good night to him, but I was sure he'd be safe on the old rug on the back porch. Mom put a wind-up alarm clock wrapped in a towel near him. She said she'd heard the ticking helped a puppy his first night away from his mother. It made me feel sad to think of Spot being taken from his mother, but I'd take him for visits. It wasn't very far away. Personally I thought Spot was too smart to be fooled by a clock in a towel but Mom wanted to do it. We all petted him and went inside to bed.

I didn't hear any more from him, but in the morning Mom and Dad said he had cried for a while before he went to sleep. Spot looked so glad to see us that I didn't think he missed his mother too much, and his brothers and sisters had all disappeared to new homes anyway, Dad had said. It was hard for Sam and me to say goodbye to him when we left for school.

The week went by fast. I played soccer with the kids every day except when it was raining, and Mark said he'd see if I could get in the league he belonged to. Every night after school I hurried home to see Spot. Mom let him in more and more because he was getting housebroken. Mark came over one night to play with him. The Stones had a dog but Mark said they'd had him as long as he could remember and that he didn't play much anymore, just lay around and slept. We had fun throwing sticks for Spot, only sometimes he'd pick up a rock instead, and he didn't always want to give the stick back so we could throw it again.

I almost managed to forget the bats, but not really. As I said, they were there in my mind, only shoved in the back underneath everything else that was going on. But sometimes they popped out whether I wanted them to or not.

Finally, on Thursday, when I was supposed to be reading my social studies book at school but was really thinking about Voro, I came to a decision. I would find out what I could from Mark about the old lady seeing the bats. I still didn't want to tell him I'd talked to them. Who'd believe a story like that? We were getting to be friends. I didn't want to blow that, in case I somehow came through all this. But I was doomed if I didn't do something. It wouldn't do any good for me to speak to the person who had talked to the old lady myself. Mom and Dad wouldn't believe me anyway. But if I told them who it was, maybe I could persuade *them* to ask about the old lady. Anyway, it was all I could think of to do.

We were walking up Mark's dirt road when I finally nerved myself to bring up the subject. "I — uh — I saw a bat the other day," I said.

"You did?" He quit kicking the stone he'd maneu- vered halfway up the driveway. His face looked interested — at first. Then he laughed. "An ordinary one? Or a big one that talked?"

"Oh, uh, just an ordinary one," I lied.

He lost interest and went back to his rock. The

toe of his shoe was getting all beat up. I knew his mother wouldn't like it. I'd heard her tell him to quit doing that.

How was I going to find out what I needed to know? I thought for a minute, then blurted out, "Where'd you hear about the old lady? I mean — that crazy story about talking bats? I think — my folks would be interested. You know, they'd think it was weird, with us living in the house and all."

"Yeah, it was wild. It was the plumber — you know, the guy you got Spot from. He was always trying to fix leaks at her — I mean, at your house. He came to our place once to help Dad put some pipes in the basement. I remember him telling about it, and Mom and Dad laughed, but then Mom said it really wasn't funny, how sad it must have been for the old lady, to live alone and get senile and everything, and imagine something gross like that."

"Yeah," I agreed.

"And the plumber said he'd known a guy in the army who kept seeing talking elephants, only he drank too much, but Mom said she knew for a fact that alcohol wasn't the old lady's problem."

"Hey," I said, "your mom's looking out the window, you'd better quit kicking —" I was glad to change the subject now that I'd found out what I wanted to know.

"Oh, yeah," he said, suddenly walking normal. "Hi, Mom!" He waved, looking innocent.

I could hardly wait to tell Mom and Dad. Just think — someone we knew had heard the story. For the first time that week I felt hopeful. I decided to wait until Dad got home. I stayed at Mark's for a while, but I kept looking at the clock. Finally I said, "I gotta go."

Mark looked surprised. "It's early."

"Yeah," I said. "Mom had some job she wanted me to do."

"Oh. Tough. Okay, I'll see you tomorrow."

Dad wasn't home when I got there. "He had to work late," Mom explained.

"Oh," I said, disappointed.

"Why?" She looked at me sharply. "You can tell me, Ricky, you know that."

I decided I would. Time was getting short. "Well, you're not going to believe this," I began, "but the old lady who lived in our house and who died —"

"Oh, Ricky," Mom interrupted, sounding sad like she always did when I brought up the subject.

"No. Wait." I was determined that somebody would believe me this time. All I was asking was that they believe the old lady had talked to the plumber, and they could ask him themselves. "Mark heard a story, and today I asked him where he'd heard it, and it was the plumber! Ours! The one we got Spot from!" My voice squeaked, I was so anxious.

Mom looked at me strangely. "Slow down, Ricky, you're not making sense. What *was* the story the old lady told the plumber we got Spot from, who told Mark who told you?"

"That the bats came. That they talked to her, too, just like they did to me!"

"Oh." That was all Mom said. She turned back to her cooking.

"Ask him," I pleaded. "Ask him, that's all I want. Will you?"

Mom didn't look at me. Her hands were busy doing something in the sink. "All right, Ricky, we'll ask," she finally said.

I waited a minute, but she didn't say anything else, so I left.

I was hoping they'd talk to the plumber that night, but they didn't. Dad was awfully late getting home, and he was tired and grumpy like he gets sometimes when he has to work overtime. I didn't want to bring up a subject that would just make it worse. It was up to Mom now. I'd done all I could when I asked Mark. I decided to really try to forget the bats for the time that was left. It would make life easier.

But it didn't work. I was reminded of the bats first thing the next morning. I'd completely forgotten about the appointment with the shrink. "I'll be picking you up at school," Mom said, "for your appointment with Dr. Jerison."

"Oh, Mom, do I have to?" I asked, but she nodded with that look that means no arguing.

It was such a waste of time, and if they'd just call the plumber we could forget the whole thing. I hoped somebody besides Mom and Dad was paying for the shrink because I knew they couldn't afford it — not when Dad had been out of work so long, and with the move. All I really wanted to do was go home and play with Spot. Mark wanted me to put him on a leash and walk him over to his house, but I lied and said I had to go to the dentist. I wasn't about to tell him where I was really going.

Dr. Jerison really knew what a person was thinking. I hadn't been with her very long before she said, "Does it make you angry to come and see me?"

I just shrugged. I was there, wasn't I? That should make everybody happy.

"Tell me about school," she said next.

I did, and we went on from there, and I told her about playing soccer. I didn't say anything about bats. I hadn't wanted to talk about them that day anyway. I'd managed to put them out of my mind and it wasn't going to do anyone any good to go on about them, especially to someone who didn't believe me.

There was a pause, and she looked at me expectantly. I mumbled something about the bats not having been back. I saw a quick flash of being pleased cross her face, as if she'd had something to do with it. I knew the bats wouldn't come this week. They'd said so, and I had told her that on my other visit. The time was getting really close when they would come again, and I didn't want to think about it before I had to, but she sure hadn't had anything to do with it.

Finally she realized I didn't have anything more to say, and Mom and I left. Mom made another appointment but I wasn't going to go again, ever. The appointment was for next week, and I might not even be around to worry about it.

I reminded Mom on the way home about the plumber. She sounded irritated when she answered me. "I *told* you we'd talk to him," she said. I shut up. Mom isn't that way often, but sometimes if you make her mad she won't do something you want that she would have done otherwise.

That night I did something I'd only done once or twice before. I eavesdropped. I knew when I went to bed that Mom and Dad were going to talk about me. I could tell by the looks they passed back and forth and the way they hustled me off to bed. I even pretended to be asleep when Mom sneaked in a few minutes later to tuck Sam and me in. It was hard to pretend, when she leaned down and kissed me like she used to when I was little, smelling the way she always does. I can tell in the dark if it's her or Dad even though I'm not sure what the difference is. Something she puts on her face, I guess. Anyway, I tried to fake heavy breathing like Sam at his best. Mom left, shutting the door behind her.

I got up right away and eased the door open. Mom and Dad were sitting in the living room talking softly, but I could hear almost every word. "Strange," Mom said. "So Terry actually said Mrs. Lewis had complained about talking bats?"

My heart thumped. They'd done it. They'd actually spoken to the plumber. I started to grin. Now maybe we'd get some action. But why hadn't they told me? I listened some more.

"It *is* strange," Dad agreed. "But the way I look at it, Ricky must have heard the story somewhere. Let's face it. He wouldn't admit it, but he's been up to Terry's house playing with the puppies practically since we got here. And his friend Mark knew — probably a lot of the kids at school —"

"But, Dick, it was the very first morning we were here — at least I think it was. Where would he already have heard a story about an old lady? Kids don't worry about old people, you know that."

Dad sighed. "I know. The whole thing stinks. I wish we'd never moved here."

"Don't say that." Mom's voice was muffled, and I

knew she was snuggled up to Dad on the couch. "You like your new job, the house is going to be great, and even Ricky's happier than he was."

"Then why doesn't he get over this obsession?" Dad asked, sounding angry. "Look, Jane. You know and I know that there's no such thing as talking bats. If we tell Ricky the plumber confirmed the story, it's just going to reinforce his behavior."

"You don't think we should tell him?" Mom's voice sounded small.

"No, I don't. We'll lie if we have to. If Ricky thinks it's been proven that the old lady saw bats, we'll never hear the end of it. Mrs. Lewis was batty herself, everyone knew that. I say we shouldn't tell him."

"Well . . ." Mom sounded hesitant. "If that's what you think — for a little while, anyway. Although it doesn't seem fair."

"It's best for Ricky. That's what we have to keep in mind." Then Dad started talking about something at work.

I felt awful, almost sick to my stomach, as I quietly shut the door and slunk back to bed. I hadn't realized how much I'd counted on Mom and Dad's talking to the plumber. It was the same old thing — they still thought I was making it all up. I'd reached the end. I'd done all the thinking I could. I'd read everything I could find, imagined all the awful things the bats could do to Sam and me, and thought about what I could do to get rid of them. No one believed me except Sam and he wasn't old enough to be any help, though I still felt good that he believed me. If he saw the bats when they came Sunday, he might be able to convince Mom and Dad that they were real. Only by then we would both be in big danger.

Now there was nothing to do but watch and wait. It would all be over soon, I knew that. Sunday was the day.

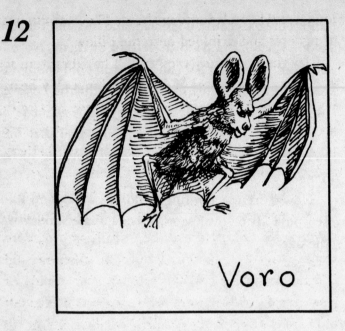

12

Voro

The humming noise began. It grew stronger. And stronger. *Oh, no,* I screamed to myself, lips tight together. *Now now — not tonight! That's not fair!*

It was only Saturday night. I'd had all these big plans for Sunday. I was going to help Mom with the dishes and Dad with my bedroom. I was going to take Spot to see his mother. I was going to play trucks with Sam. If Sunday was going to be my last day I wanted everyone to remember the good things I did, not the bad. I thought of all the times I'd worried Mom and Dad or made them mad. I thought about the times I hadn't wanted to play with Sam, or had teased him. All the while the humming grew louder and pounded into my head. The tears ran out of my eyes and dribbled onto the pillow.

I lay there with my eyes shut. The vibes were so strong my head felt as if it would burst. My heart pounded and my pajamas were already wet with sweat. Maybe that's all the bats had to do — scare me to death, as they had the old lady. I felt halfway there. Do kids my age ever die of heart attacks?

I waited for whatever was going to happen, ignoring Voro who, I knew, would be hanging upside-down in his usual place at the foot of my bed. Voro wouldn't like being ignored, but what difference did it make now? The vibes, or vibrations or sounds, or whatever they were, were the strongest I'd ever felt or heard. As before, they came in waves, building up to a point where I had to put my hands over my ears (which didn't do any good at all) and screw my face up to keep from screaming out loud.

I remembered my promise to Sam to wake him up to see the bats. No, it was too late for that. This time they meant business. It wouldn't do to remind them about Sam. Maybe if he stayed asleep they would forget all about him and I could at least save Sam. That made me feel a little better, but not much.

I thought of going ahead and screaming. The bats would disappear and Mom and Dad would come in and look at me with sad faces and I'd be right back where I'd been. Worrying, and not being able to sleep, and getting dragged off to the shrink. No, I might as well get it over with.

Voro began to talk to me. "We gave you your chance to get out of our house. Why are you still here?"

"*Why are you still here? Why are you still here?*" the other bats chorused like some weird song.

I bit my lip and didn't answer. One of the bats dove for my face. I could feel it coming. I winced, but at the last minute he missed. The passing air felt cold on my wet skin.

"It won't do you any good not to answer me," Voro said in a quiet voice. Not *nice* quiet — *mean* quiet. Then he shouted, "*Answer me! Why are you still in our house?*"

I slowly opened my eyes. Just as I expected, Voro hung in his usual place. The only difference from the other night was that this time the room was filled, packed with bats. I didn't know there were so many bats in the world. No, that's not true, I knew; but if they'd all flown out the window at the same time, it would look like pictures I'd seen of Carlsbad Caverns. There were bats hanging from every possible thing they could attach themselves to — my bed, Sam's bed, the molding around the ceiling, the pictures. There were even bats hanging from bats. In the middle of it all, Sam slept like the dead. That wasn't a good way of putting it. I didn't need to think about dead people right then.

"I told you," I answered, carefully avoiding looking in Sam's direction. I tried once more to convince Voro how hopeless it was. "No one believes me." If only I could keep him from thinking about Sam and remembering that he had threatened to go after my brother.

I didn't know an animal could get so many expressions on its face. First a skeptical look crossed Voro's ugly features, then an unbelieving one. Finally anger made his lips draw back, showing even more ferocious teeth than I'd seen before, and his eyes became mere slits as he glared at me. From being angry, he progressed to furious. All the while I stared as if hypnotized, and I waited to see what he would do. I couldn't force myself not to look into the fierce black eyes that stared at me upside-down. My body was shivering and I tried to keep the bed from shaking. It wouldn't do to have Voro aware of how scared I was. But since he seemed to read my mind anyway, I probably wasn't fooling him one bit.

Then he gave a signal. I didn't hear a sound and he didn't flap his wings or duck his head or anything like that, but somehow he sent a message, because instantaneously all the bats let go of whatever they were clinging to and began to fly. It was some sight.

The bedroom wasn't very big, and all those hundreds — maybe thousands — of bats flying around in there without ever running into each other was hard to believe.

They weren't moving in any pattern, like planes circling an airport all in the same direction. They just flew any which way, dodging and maneuvering and missing each other by no more than the thickness of their skin. I didn't see how they could do it, but then I remembered reading in the bat book about how they send out waves of sound that we can't hear but they can, and the sounds bounce back from objects so that they know not to bump into anything. Submarines use something like that underwater but bats had the idea first. Maybe their sound waves were what I felt when they were around.

For a second I was so fascinated I forgot to be scared. But then Voro must have given another signal because their flight did begin to have an aim. Me. They started flying straight toward me, each of them with a mean grimace only a little less terrifying than Voro's. They dove at me one by one and then in clumps, all of them with mouths open. Their black eyes showed flashes of red reflected from the night-light and their faces were gruesome, with the extra folds of skin and what looked like double ears. I whimpered and ducked, flopped over on my stomach, and hid my head in my arms.

I forgot to be glad they were attacking me instead of Sam. I cowered and felt the pillow under my face get soggy with sweat and tears. If I thought my heart had been thumping hard before, now it seemed loud enough to wake Sam. The blood pounded in my head, and I waited to feel teeth sink into my neck or claws dig into my shoulder.

I must have been holding my breath; I felt dizzy until I realized I needed to breathe out. When I sucked in a breath I almost gagged. There was an odd smell — musky and damp, like the basement in an old, abandoned house. The bats still dove at me. I could feel the rush of air and the stronger vibrations as they approached, but still no fangs had found blood. I quivered, and waited some more.

Then I remembered Sam. With my head buried I couldn't tell what else was going on in the room. Was Voro one of those diving at me or was he still hanging there directing traffic? And had some of that traffic been sent Sam's way? I heard Sam whimper and my heart really sank. I was going to have to quit lying there like a jellyfish stranded on the sand and nerve myself to find out what was going on. I opened my eyes.

That didn't help much since I was still scrunched down on my stomach with my back to the action. I took a deep breath, then another. All the while, the din of the vibrations of all those bats kept me from

107

concentrating. Maybe it was just as well. If I'd really thought I would have had more sense than to do what I did — roll over and swing my arms at the diving bats the way you do to make a yellow jacket go away.

I raised my head and looked around. Sam was still asleep, and the bats were ignoring him. The noise he made must have been just one of the usual ones he makes when dreaming. Quickly I switched my eyes to the foot of the bed. Voro was still there, bouncing up and down he was so mad. He flexed his wings, folding and unfolding them as he shouted, "Die, die!" He was echoed with a screech by all the bats in the room.

The bats had backed off when I swung, but now they began their dives again. I swatted at one, and it worked. He missed my arm at the last minute just like he missed his brothers in the air. I began to have a tiny bit of hope. I remembered how quietly Voro had talked before he got so mad, and I decided to try to do that, too. I wasn't exactly brave, but I could pretend to be. "No one believes me," I told him again, "no one at all. And even if they believed me, why should we move?"

My voice got louder, I couldn't help it. "We bought this house. It's ours! Not yours! Why don't *you* get out of *our* house?" I was shouting now. Who did they think they were, anyway? The bats were surprised and so was I. Had I actually stood up to them? Maybe when a person pretended to be brave it helped to make the bravery real.

The bats didn't like it. They quit diving at me but they fluttered in agitation and some of them settled on their perches again. *"It's ours, it's ours!"* they shrieked. They didn't sound as sure of themselves as they had. I suddenly felt even braver. I sat up in bed.

The bats hadn't done anything to me. I was still alive. For all those menacing teeth, none of the bats had bitten me, or clawed me, or for that matter even touched me. I felt the cold air as they whizzed past, but that was all. Was it possible that that was all they could do — try to scare a person to death? It had worked on the old lady, that I was sure of, but maybe her heart had been worn out anyway.

"We'll just have to go after your brother," Voro snarled, and I suddenly was scared again. "I warned you. The old ones will believe us then!"

"His brother, his brother," the other bats chanted. Then, again at a signal from Voro, they left me entirely and switched to poor Sam. They spread their wings, veering and wheeling like a dark cloud. As they dove, I sat there stunned, hoping he wouldn't wake up. The bats might not know how soundly he

slept. Sam moaned and flopped over on his side, and I thought I saw a bat catch his claws in Sam's hair. Was I wrong about their not actually being able to touch and hurt a person? It was happening so fast I couldn't make up my mind what to do.

Even if I weren't wrong, Sam might be so scared that his heart would give out. He was so little he'd never had to be brave — he hadn't had any practice. Maybe he could be frightened so badly that he *would* die. Sam whimpered again and rubbed one hand across his face as if he were waking up.

Whatever happened to me, I couldn't let the bats hurt Sam. "Oh, no you don't!" I was mad. "You aren't going to pick on him. I won't *let* you!" Voro hissed and spread his wings menacingly. He looked twice as big as I'd ever seen him. Was he going to come after me himself? I had to go, anyway. I threw back the covers and jumped up, brushing bats out of the way as I ran to Sam's bed. "Pick on somebody your own size!" I yelled, knowing that I wasn't making sense but not caring. I put my hands on my hips with my elbows sticking out. I don't know why except I thought it would look tough. It made me *feel* tough!

For the first time, Voro himself didn't appear so confident. I'd moved on the other side of the foot rail, and he had to crane his neck to see me. He looked uncomfortable, and I hoped he was. I felt stronger and stronger. I also, I was surprised to find, felt bigger. Voro didn't look nearly as large now that I was staring down at him. Standing up and defying them sure beat quivering in bed, waiting.

Some of the bats were still diving at my brother and I couldn't help ducking even though I was pretty sure they would miss me. Sam mumbled something about bats in his sleep, and I whispered imploringly, "Don't wake up!" Most of the bats had quit diving, I realized, and had returned to their perches on the pictures and molding and curtain rods. The bats that were still charging were particularly vicious ones that didn't look as if they frightened easily.

I picked up one of Sam's shoes, which were lying, as they always do, right where he'd dropped them beside the bed. I wasn't planning to *kill* a bat. I couldn't do that. I couldn't kill anything. That is, unless I had to, to protect Sam. I gritted my teeth and waved the shoe in front of me.

"Don't you *dare* come after Sam," I ordered, "or I'll come after you."

Voro stared at me, amazed. Maybe he wasn't used to being faced up to. We stared at each other, neither of us blinking, just like the first time I saw him. Then, before I even knew what I was doing, I threw the shoe. I reached down quickly and picked up the other in case I needed it, but I didn't. My aim had been good — the shoe had flown across the room and bonked Voro a good one.

I'd *hit* him. I'd really done it. I'd knocked him off his perch on the foot of my bed. I put down the other shoe. "Are you hurt?" I asked as I started toward the small, black lump that was Voro.

"*Hurt, hurt, hurt,*" the bats cried.

"You did it, you did it!" I jumped a mile when Sam screeched and threw his arms around my neck from behind. I sagged onto the bed. "You didn't wake me up, though," His voice was accusing. "I woke myself up."

"I didn't want —" I looked over my shoulder at Sam, who was bouncing on the bed. He looked perfectly fine but I asked, just in case, "Are you okay?" I thought about the fangs and teeth. "They didn't bite you, or —"

"Nah, they didn't touch me. I see them, I see them too!" He was really excited.

A bat whizzed by me, and I turned quickly back to the action. As I watched, a cloud of bats whirled overhead and then began trickling away in a gray fog. Suddenly there weren't as many in the room. A couple of the remaining ones fluttered down to Voro, who started moving before I could get to him, then staggered up to his old spot on the foot of my bed. "*He hit Voro, he's too brave,*" the bats were all saying together.

Who, me?

Voro wasn't saying it. He was a mean one to the end. He didn't say anything, just glared at me. But the glare was different. *He* was afraid of *me*. Me, who can't kill a fly.

Sam came up behind me again, his mouth near my ear. "Why don't you catch him, Ricky? You could keep him for a pet," he whispered.

Catch him? Could I? He didn't look nearly so fierce as before; instead, he was rumpled and shaky. If I caught him, everyone would know I'd been telling the truth. Mom and Dad and Dr. Jerison. Sam knew, now, and I was glad. I could show Voro to Mark, and maybe take him to school. I looked around quickly, trying to figure out how I could do it.

Sam's jacket was lying on the foot of his bed. Slyly, without taking my eyes off Voro, I reached for the jacket. My hand moved slowly, and I pulled it across the bed toward me. If I moved fast while Voro was still discombobulated, maybe I could do it. I twitched my shoulders so Sam would let go and whispered back, "Shhh!"

Then I pounced. I threw the jacket over Voro,

and scrunched it carefully into a bundle. Inside, Voro struggled, his wings flapping in an effort to fly.

"You *got* him!" Sam hollered, and overhead the remaining bats flew in an agitated circle. I watched to be sure they didn't dive at either of us, but they didn't. In my hands, Voro's little body continued to struggle.

It was then that I began to feel sorry for him. What would happen if I kept him? I didn't know what he ate so I wouldn't be able to feed him. Worse yet, what if Mom and Dad wanted to kill him? The bats overhead were frightened for him, I could tell. He was their leader.

And why keep him, anyway? Just to prove something? I didn't need that. Sam would tell Mom and Dad, and that was enough.

"If I let you go," I said to Voro, who had given up the fight and lay limp under Sam's jacket, "will you promise to go away and leave us alone?"

He agreed. I could sense it, the same way I knew everything else he said.

A thought came to me. "And you'll promise not to bother other people either? No more threatening humans — you'll take the rest of the bats and go away?" I kept my hand on him carefully, still not trusting him.

He gave one agitated lurch. Voro was, after all,

still Voro. Finally, with obvious reluctance, he said in our strange way of communicating, "I promise."

Somehow I knew I could believe him. He hadn't wanted to agree, but once he did, he'd live up to his promise. I whipped the jacket off. Without another word, Voro gathered himself together and took to the air. I realized it was the first time I'd seen him actually fly. He swooped around the room a time or two, the other bats encircling him. None of them looked as large as they had.

"*He's too brave,*" the bats kept repeating. Not Voro, naturally; just his buddies, as if they were trying to convince him of something. If they'd only known how scared I really was they wouldn't have said that.

Beside me now, Sam watched. "Wow!" he exclaimed.

Suddenly Voro broke away from the pack and flew directly in front of me, our eyes meeting for a brief second. His were no longer fierce, but bewildered and lost. Then the bats gave one last swoop and disappeared. Voro, his mean buddies, and all the rest. They were gone forever.

Just as they took their final loop, I heard a strangled gasp behind me. I swung around to see Mom, her fists to her mouth and her eyes popping. She held out her arms, and I went to her. "It's okay,

Mom," I tried to reassure her. "They're gone." She hugged me, crying, and Sam cheered, and just then Dad showed up, rubbing his eyes and wanting to know what was going on. It sure made me feel good to see the expressions on their faces.

I decided I'd tell one more person — Mark. I thought he'd be interested in my bat story.

HOWLING GOOD FUN
FROM AVON CAMELOT

Meet the 5th graders of P.S. 13—
the craziest, creepiest kids ever!

M IS FOR MONSTER
                    75423-1/$2.75 US/$3.25 CAN
by Mel Gilden; illustrated by John Pierard

BORN TO HOWL   75425-8/$2.50 US/$3.25 CAN
by Mel Gilden; illustrated by John Pierard

THERE'S A BATWING IN MY
    LUNCHBOX   75426-6/$2.75 US/$3.25 CAN
by Ann Hodgman; illustrated by John Pierard

THE PET OF FRANKENSTEIN
        75185-2/$2.50 US/$2.50 US/$3.25 CAN
by Mel Gilden; illustrated by John Pierard

Z IS FOR ZOMBIE 75686-2/$2.75 US/$3.25 CAN
by Mel Gilden; illustrated by John Pierard